ROLL OVER PLAY DEAD

ROLL OVER PLAY DEAD

Vivien Armstrong

This first world edition published in Great Britain 2007 by
SEVERN HOUSE PUBLISHERS LTD of
9–15 High Street, Sutton, Surrey SM1 1DF.
This first world edition published in the USA 2007 by
SEVERN HOUSE PUBLISHERS INC of
595 Madison Avenue, New York, N.Y. 10022.

British Library Cataloguing in Publication Data

Armstrong, Vivien
    Roll over, play dead. - (A Detective Chief Inspector Roger Hayes mystery)
    1. Hayes, Roger (Fictitious character) - Fiction
    2. Police - England - Fiction
    3. Detective and mystery stories
    I. Title
    823.9'14 [F]

    ISBN-13: 978-0-7278-6484-0

Typeset by Palimpsest Book Production Ltd.,
Grangemouth, Stirlingshire, Scotland.
Printed and bound in Great Britain by
MPG Books Ltd., Bodmin, Cornwall.

One

When Suzie Brigham's naked body was found at the bottom of the stairs, it was at first assumed that the slim redhead had simply tripped. There was no indication of an intruder, no evidence of a robbery and Bill Wickham, her estate manager, the man who had discovered the body, confided in the duty sergeant that, 'Well, to be honest, the lady liked a dram or two.'

But when the doctor arrived and the victim was turned over, the marks of a vicious beating were all too clear.

Detective Inspector Trevor Clarke got straight through to headquarters. The Brighams were not to be trifled with and if the local gossip about Sir William's new wife was to be taken into account, the case would require a sensitivity Clarke was far from certain he could handle. Aspern Grange and the grounds were immediately sealed off, and Bill Wickham was driven to the local nick before the news broke on the lunchtime TV bulletin. Clarke instructed his driver to put his foot down and speeded to Horsham to report to the top brass.

Detective Superintendent Roger Hayes was already disenchanted by three months' secondment to the Met's new squad. Even the leapfrog promotion had lost its shine, the lure of a whole new intelligence unit under his command so far proving little more than a hyped-up think tank dreamed up in a government panic move to allay voters' dissatisfaction with crime statistics.

They had given him a smart office in Pimlico, an anonymous building in a set of rooms appropriate to the new crack force comprising two detective constables, an IT specialist called Maurice Gibson and a sergeant, Morwenna Prentice, chosen Hayes could only imagine for her strapping physique, which would, in the event of any roughhouse, be as good as having his own pet Rottweiler. Hayes' recent mugging, which had resulted in a lengthy convalescence and subsequent transfer to this so-called intelligence unit, was a story he had hoped would have died the death by now, the attack having occurred on an off-duty excursion earning him only ribald and jealous comment from fellow officers. Being shunted from DCI to detective superintendent and given a cushy sinecure as a result of a stupid encounter with street yobs had turned sour.

Hayes reluctantly had to admit he had only two options: to leave the force and try something else, or accept this desk job which, with a competent team, he might eventually organize into a decent national investigative system. The idea, deeply resented in the shires, was to form a team of specialized CID officers who could be called on for any high-profile cases with special regard to national security. So far Hayes had spent fruitless weeks tacking between Westminster and Scotland Yard in an effort to put parameters on the exact nature of the job.

Mo Prentice stuck her head round the door. 'The Commander wants you upstairs, sir.'

Hayes spun round, startled from his concentration on two pigeons bickering on the windowsill over the remains of his lunchtime cheese sandwich.

'Eh? What did you say?'

'The Commander,' she patiently repeated, her hazel eyes narrowing. Prentice had, according to her file, enjoyed considerable success in the Serious Fraud Office before being seconded to Hayes' private army, and was, Hayes guessed, as impatient with the nebulous quality of this new job as he himself, her irritation often boiling over in the computer room. He was still interviewing recruits, and so far this new hit squad, as he personally regarded it, had hardly dipped its toe in the water.

Two

Commander Crick's door stood open, the unheated room suffused with pale sunlight that gamely struggled to bring an element of warmth to the chill. Hayes paused on the threshold and straightened his tie, wondering if Alex Crick's spurning of central heating on this miserable autumn afternoon was some sort of macho stance or a sop to the environmental lobby.

The boss man looked up from his desk and motioned Hayes to close the door. His sidekick, a pasty-faced senior officer from the Security Service called Bennet, eyed Hayes, Crick's flavour of the month, with disfavour.

'Ah, Hayes. You have met Superintendent Bennet? Yes, well, pull up a chair. We've an emergency on our hands and Bennet suggests you might be just the man to handle it.'

Hayes sat down and dismally conjectured that if there was a pile of shit to be shifted, it was no surprise that Bennet had put his name top of the list. Frequent run-ins with Steve Bennet had invariably foundered on the exact purpose of this new intelligence unit, currently dubbed 'Melrose'. Neither of them was entirely sure, and Bennet was increasingly anxious that the remit did not overlap his own little fiefdom.

Hayes waited while Crick took a phone call, his curt responses giving nothing away. He glanced around the room, which bore no personal touches whatsoever, not so much as a framed certificate on the wall or even a bloody fishing trophy. Crick's desk was devoid of paperwork or the usual paraphernalia of one-upmanship: no executive toys for a start and certainly no silver ashtray. Hayes nervously patted the cigarettes in his jacket pocket and waited for the Commander to finish the call.

'Ah, yes, Hayes – where were we? Now, this little matter we would like you to attend to is, Bennet thinks, right up your street, bearing in mind your previous experience of murder investigations with the Thames Valley force. However—'

'There is a security aspect to the case,' Bennet blurted out, 'which requires sensitive handling.'

Hayes raised an eyebrow. 'Indeed?'

This cool response goaded Crick to raise a hand, cutting off Bennet's retort.

'To summarize the situation, Hayes . . .' He paused, glancing down at pencilled notes. 'The wife of a valuable government official has been bludgeoned to death. In her own home,' he added gravely – as if this could be a comfort to the poor woman, Hayes sourly concluded.

'And where was this, sir?'

'At their country house, in a village called Flodde, near Horsham. Sussex. The young woman was found at ten o'clock this morning and the local team were anxious not to embarrass Sir William, the husband, who is in Brussels, and who—'

'Sir William Brigham,' Bennet snapped.

Hayes brightened. 'The pharmaceutical buff recently brought in to head up the EU Medical Coordination Unit?'

'Exactly so,' Crick put in, anxious to keep Bennet on a close rein, a man whose impatience threatened to take control of the interview. Hayes stifled a grin, regarding this tug of war with bemusement. Crick, he had already decided, was a good administrator but easily hustled. 'Glad to see you're up to speed already, Hayes. Good man.' Crick gave a wintry smile and accepted a bulky envelope from Bennet, which he shoved across the desk to Hayes smartish as if it was a letter bomb.

Hayes sighed. He'd been right. Bennet's pile of shit had indeed come his way.

'It's all in the file – as much as we've got so far, Hayes. Your liaison officer at Horsham is a Detective Superintendent Fox. You will work closely with the local man, DI . . . ?'

'Clarke.'

'Ah, yes, thank you, Bennet. Detective Inspector Clarke. But in view of the inevitable media interest, we shall have to handle it with kid gloves. Bennet will go over the file with you in his office and pinpoint the political angles. Take that young officer with you, Sergeant Prentice, it will be good experience for her.'

Hayes rose. 'Yes, sir. But Prentice is a fraud expert. Is that relevant?'

Crick waved a dismissive hand and threw back his head in exasperation. 'How the hell would I know, Hayes? Just get on with it, man. Like I told you, this is an emergency.'

Three

The run-through in Bennet's office was brief and to the point. Suzannah Brigham, thirty-two years old and a former model, was a stunner, no question. Bennet had already procured several glamour shots of the victim and as the contents of the envelope spilled out onto the conference table, including a bunch of press cuttings relating to Sir William, Hayes had to admit the bloke was no slouch.

The three seated themselves round the table, Bennet presiding. Hayes' Rottweiler, Mo Prentice, was breathing heavily, barely holding back an urge to grab the printouts. It was, Hayes guessed, her first shot at a murder enquiry and the girl's enthusiasm prompted him, after a quick shuffle through the file, to accept that Bennet's 'pile of shit' was, in fact, an interesting case.

Crick's security expert concentrated on the high profile of the unfortunate widower. 'A low-key approach is paramount,' he insisted, his sallow features flushing with determination. The fact that MI5 was involved in what might turn out to be a bungled burglary implied that Bennet's envelope was short on background music. But even after only two months in the new job, Hayes had learned that once any security angle was involved, even a more senior man than himself would be restricted by a 'need to know' basis.

Perhaps Bennet's touchiness about Sir William cloaked embarrassing facts which the powers that be would prefer to remain hidden. But any murder investigation would inevitably dig the dirt and any murky details applied to the man himself or to his unfortunate wife would surely come under the spotlight despite any defensive moves from Hayes' unit.

Hayes rather doubted whether even he, with the backup

of Commander Crick, could dispute any fallout, and if, as he suspected, Bennet had given him only half the story, it would be *his* head on the block if the case turned sour. Not a jolly prospect for the first test case to come his way.

Hayes let Bennet have his head, listening patiently without interruption to the official line. Mo Prentice took notes, her clear appreciation of Bennet's grasp of the case cooling the prevailing atmosphere between the two men.

'Suzannah Brigham, née Anstruther, previously married to a photographer called Fritz Grice,' Bennet quoted from the file.

'Yeah, Grice is big time. *Vogue. Harper's.* Hauled in for heroin abuse two years ago but still in demand.'

'Ah, then I needn't join up the dots, Superintendent,' Bennet sourly retorted.

'My ex was a magazine editor. I used to get all that crap with my breakfast cornflakes.'

'Divorced?'

'Absolutely.'

'Then you won't quibble about overtime. Not that this little problem needs to impinge on the weekend. It's just that we must shield our man from any press intrusion as much as possible.'

Prentice leaned forward. 'Sir William has been informed?'

'He's on his way back from Brussels now. But MI5 insist on intervening. They're sending a car, a discreet pick-up at City Airport. They're anxious to keep the media at bay for as long as possible. A pretty woman found dead at the bottom of her stairs is like flypaper to the tabloid hacks.' He paused, studying the glossy pics spread across his desk, Suzannah Brigham's sun-kissed thighs provocatively posed against a backdrop of sand dunes. He coughed and shuffled the photographs back into the envelope. 'We suggest you, Hayes, and Prentice book into a B&B in the vicinity. Got the message? Low profile!'

Hayes nodded. 'I'll sift through these notes,' he said, gathering up the loose paperwork from the table, 'and get back to you as soon as I've made a few phone calls. And when—'

Bennet rose, cutting Hayes off short. 'Well, don't waste time on this, Hayes. A quick recce should do it.'

Hayes' mouth took on a comic downturn as he ushered Prentice into his office. They spent less than twenty minutes going over the file and, after confirming their arrangements with the hapless DI Clarke, drove straight to Horsham.

Superintendent Fox, the man in the firing line now that the news had broken, occupied an L-shaped room on the quieter side of the station. Hayes relaxed, recognizing an experienced copper lacking Bennet's paranoia. Fox greeted the two interlopers from the Met with a friendly nod and wasted no time getting down to details.

'DI Clarke is supervising the case but we have delayed the transfer of the body to the mortuary as you will doubtless wish to examine the crime scene before any disturbance. My SOC officers have completed their investigation and the surgeon has made an initial examination. The dead woman appears to have been attacked at least ten hours before she was discovered.'

Hayes nodded, surprised that the arrival of two senior officers from the new Melrose Unit had been accepted without demur. From Bennet's brief notes it would seem Sir William's country house was adequately burglar-proofed but the lack of evidence of any intruder would need closer examination.

'Was there any local controversy involving the Brighams, sir?' Prentice put in. 'A boundary dispute? Scandal? Gossip?'

Superintendent Fox drew back, clearly dismayed at the innuendo. 'The Brighams were well liked,' he stiffly replied. 'Lady Brigham was a fine horsewoman and had taken an interest in the pony club. Encouraged the youngsters a good deal . . .' he lamely added.

Hayes rose and unceremoniously pushed his sergeant towards the door. 'We'll go straight to the house, Superintendent. We don't want to keep your man waiting.'

Mo Prentice accepted his car keys with a mulish flick of her head, and Hayes suppressed a mild reproof. If they were to work together on this he would have to spell out his working methods to this woman, but not yet. He was keen that there be no sort of showdown at this early stage. First things first. 'An emergency', the Commander had insisted. It was vital to get at the crime scene before the local plod stamped all over it.

He soon realized that if there was a lack of finesse in Prentice's detection skills she was, he had to acknowledge, a bloody good driver. They covered the distance to the Grange at top speed and without so much as a blink at the map.

Four

Aspern Grange proved to be a small manor house set in several acres of land. Sheep grazed in an adjoining field and a stable block dominated a fenced-off area next to the walled garden to the west front. From the road a wide farm gate gave on to a gravelled drive that led through scrubby woodland to the main entrance. It was, at first glance, a mixed-up property, undecided whether to continue its earlier heritage as a Victorian farmhouse or toe a more fashionable line as gentleman's country bolt-hole.

A uniformed constable stepped forward to examine Hayes' ID before Prentice drove on at a more decorous pace, giving them both the opportunity to take in the scene. Dusk had already fallen and dark rain clouds hung low over a gabled building set snugly amid the trees.

'Nice place,' Hayes remarked as they stepped out onto a forecourt where two police cars and a mortuary van were parked. Prentice perked up as they approached the door, clearly a girl whose basic good nature harboured no extended moody blues, he was pleased to note.

Inside, a section of the square hallway was taped off, the body temporarily covered by a plastic sheet provided by the SOCO team. A plainclothes guy, presumably Clarke's sergeant, scuttled off to fetch his boss while they waited.

Hayes gazed around with interest. The staircase was uncarpeted; the oak risers were steeper than those of modern steps and to Hayes' critical eye probably something to get used to. He wondered if there was a set of back stairs connected to the kitchen which would probably be more frequently used. The old farmhouse had been extended and modernized to accommodate all the mod cons but the conversion had been cleverly managed if first impressions were any indication.

DI Clarke bustled in: a short figure running to middle-age spread but pleasant enough and seeming to harbour no anxiety as to the arrival of two Met officers to check out the security aspect.

Clarke invited Hayes to view the body and waited while the unfortunate Suzannah Brigham was subjected to yet another intrusive examination. Dark stains spattered the wainscot and a pool of blood had congealed between the flagstones. The figure spreadeagled at the bottom of the staircase looked unreal, too much like a broken shop mannequin, the skin pale as alabaster and faintly luminous. Tousled auburn hair half-concealed her face but the rouged lips, stridently scarlet, gaped, forming an ugly grimace in death, spoiling what Hayes knew to have been classically beautiful features. She wore a single gold sandal, its stiletto heel sharp as a pin, thin straps crossing narrow feet. Its twin lay halfway up the stairs, waiting, Hayes fancifully conjectured, to join its mate.

The afternoon light had now entirely faded and the illumination in the windowless hall was dim. Hayes produced a torch and crouched down to peer at her injuries.

'Was this how she was found?'

'We have pictures of the original crime scene but the doctor turned her over. Bashed over the back of the head, poor woman. More than once, Doctor Cameron says, though the pathologist will have more information when they get her on the slab, of course.'

'Weapon?'

'Possibly.'

Clarke bent down to join Hayes and pointed to matted red hair clogging a deep wound in the skull. 'Difficult to be sure, sir, but there was this shillelagh a few feet away. Being tested for bloodstains, they rushed it straight to the lab.'

'A what?'

'A shillelagh. Irish, I think – a heavy blackthorn stick, knobbly. A useful weapon, which according to Mr Wickham,

the man who found her this morning, was usually kept in
the umbrella stand by the front door.' He pointed to a blue-
and-white Chinese-style pot containing a couple of walking
sticks and a golf umbrella. 'More of a curiosity, Wickham
thought, an antique piece which used to hang in the gun
room but Sir William took a fancy to it and polished it up
himself before it was brought in here. Used to show it off
to his guests, jokingly referred to it as his caveman's club.'

'So she didn't simply fall downstairs?'

'Not necessarily, sir, but the doctor thought it unlikely.'

Hayes turned to Prentice. 'Come on, girl, what's your
take on this? A woman hears a noise downstairs. Would
she grab something like this shillelagh to defend herself?'

Prentice shook her head. 'Wouldn't be my idea to wait
till I got down here to pick up a stick, but who can say?
The obvious thing would have been to make an emergency
phone call from the bedroom – unless, of course, she was
expecting someone.'

'Maybe she wasn't in the bedroom. Maybe she was about
to get in the bath.'

'There is a shower off the gun room . . .' Clarke doubt-
fully put in.

'But to open the door without putting something on,'
Prentice doggedly pursued.

Hayes shrugged. 'Girls do. My ex made a habit of fetching
the morning paper from the box outside our front door in the
nuddies. The milkman spotted her one time. Made his day.'

Clarke laughed. 'I bet!'

'Anything known about the lady? A boyfriend? A cat to
be put out at night?'

'Nothing concrete. No pets apart from three horses in the
stables which the farm manager deals with.'

'Wickham.'

'Yes. Seems a straight-up sort but I expect you would
like a word, sir. He lives in the staff cottage round the back.'

'Married?'

'No. Got a live-in girlfriend, though, someone from the
village, just a kid really. Tracey Wilson. Too young for a
bloke like Wickham but he's a charmer all right.'

'Any local gossip?'

Clarke paused, eyeing Mo Prentice with apprehension, anxious not to cause offence to someone who looked as if she might have strong feminist sympathies. 'Well, there was a spat in the village post office last week with Sir William's ex-wife, still calls herself Lady Brigham and lives only three miles down the road, practically on the doorstep.'

Hayes grinned. 'Catfight?'

'Bitter words. Bound to happen, moving into a place as close as that. The first Lady Brigham's grown-up daughter spends weekends with her there so I heard and has taken her mother's side since the divorce. The fur's bound to fly, living within spitting distance of the old home.'

This interesting bit of background was interrupted by the arrival of a harassed mortuary attendant. 'Any hope of getting this job done, mate? The husband's due at the mortuary shortly and my boss wants to have a dekko before the lady goes on parade.'

Clarke deferred to Hayes. 'OK by you, sir?'

'Sure. Perhaps you could show me round, Inspector. Any information about incoming phone calls last night?'

'Not yet, sir, but my sergeant is checking.'

'Right. Well, I think my sergeant here and I have seen enough at present.' He turned to Prentice and said, 'Perhaps you could chase up this farm manager chap, see what he's got to say, eh?'

She closed her notebook and turned on her heel, brusquely brushing past the mortuary attendant as if the poor guy was some sort of body-snatcher.

Hayes followed Clarke upstairs, admiring the elaborately carved banisters that did, on reflection, seem a bit over the top for a Victorian farmhouse. But in the passage of time and in the course of the rising status of Aspern Grange, it had presumably been gussied up even before Sir William and his lovely new wife had a go at it.

Five

Mo Prentice left Hayes to it and made a beeline for the staff cottage at the back of the stables. Hayes' assessment of his new assistant had been hyper-critical. True, she was tall, not far short of six feet at a guess. One might almost call her statuesque, but the impression of a severe Swedish gymnast persisted, augmented he imagined by the cycle commute to the office from her flat in Vauxhall. Hayes ruefully wondered if it was her lack of appreciation of his black humour that had bugged him, or merely her cool appraisal of his style of investigation, an unspoken raising of the eyebrow which flicked him on the raw.

She wore corduroy slacks and a red ski jacket, her dark blonde hair tied back in a ponytail, a fresh complexion complementing her most attractive feature: wide greenish hazel eyes. An English Brünnhilde about covered it.

She picked her way along a muddy path to the cottage door and knocked. The curtains remained open and the lamp-lit interior glowed. A girl opened the door, a skinny kid no more than a teenager at a glance, her slight frame silhouetted against the bright backdrop.

Prentice flashed her ID card and asked for Wickham.

'Bill's not back yet. Down at the nick in Horsham.'

'Still being interviewed?'

She shrugged. 'S'pose so. Want to wait inside?'

Mo smiled. 'That would be nice. You must be Tracey.'

The girl nodded and led the way through. The front door opened straight into the overheated sitting room where a cast-iron log burner bounced heat off the walls, a pine table strewn with mugs and account books occupying a good deal of the small living area.

'Like a cuppa, miss?' Tracey said, smiling shyly, seeming glad of a bit of company.

'Thanks. I bet you've been worried about strangers hanging about the place since the accident.'

'Suzie *is* dead, ain't she? Bill didn't say it was an accident. You reckon she just fell down the stairs, then?'

'No idea. Has Bill phoned you since he was driven off to the station?'

Tracey shrugged narrow shoulders and turned away, reaching for clean mugs on the dresser.

Prentice decided to change tack. 'Been living here long, Tracey?'

'Coupla months.' She tossed tea bags into a pot and pushed the account books aside. 'Sugar?'

'No thanks. You're from the village?'

'My mum lives in a caravan behind the smithy. With my little brothers.'

'Not far away, then. You see them most days, I expect.'

Tracey slumped into a chair. 'She don't want me round since I took up with Bill. Hates his guts, she does.'

'Rotten luck – bet you miss your little brothers, though.'

'It was bloody crowded all of us in that shitty caravan. We used to have a council house but we got shoved out. Mum got behind with the rent . . .' She grinned. 'It's nicer here.'

'And Bill's OK?'

'Treats me like a princess and I get to do a bit of cleaning at the big house. Help Mrs Cosham.'

'Is that the housekeeper?'

'She don't live in no more. Not since Suzie come. Suzie don't like staff living in the house, prefers her privacy, see, 'specially as Mrs C. used to work for Sir William's old wife before the divorce.'

'You knew the previous Lady Brigham?'

'Blimey, yes. A right old bag an' all. Not surprised he got shot of her and married Suzie.'

'You liked Suzie?'

Tracey's face broke into a wide grin. '*Everyone* liked Suzie. She was really nice.' Her lip quivered. 'Don't know what'll 'appen now she's gone. Sir William's away a lot as it is. It was Suzie who loved it here. Because of the horses.'

'Horses?'

'Yeah. Three great big hunters. One of 'em's Eva's.'

Mo raised an eyebrow. 'Eva?'

'His daughter. Works in London all week but comes down most weekends and stays at her mum's new 'ouse in the next village.'

'But Eva comes here to the Grange to ride?'

'Not if Suzie's around. Won't come near Sir William neither but rides when they're both away. Bill looks after the horses and lets me ride Eva's Denzil when no one's here. There's no stables at the old girl's place, so to keep the peace her father lets Eva play it her way. Suzie reckoned Eva would come round in time.'

'Eva didn't take to her stepmother?'

'No way. Though what there was to dislike beats me. It's because her mum's so bitter about the split-up, I s'pose.'

'Puts Eva in a difficult position?'

'Well, it don't cause Renny any loss of sleep! He's here often enough. The son,' she added. 'Though Renny only turns up when he's short of cash, according to Bill.'

'Renny lives in London too?'

'Yeah. He's some sort of personal trainer, Bill says.' She laughed. 'A muscle man.'

'Not 'alf. Takes rich ladies for a jog in the park, and that's only the start, Bill reckons.' She snorted, grinning like a cheeky kid, her impish face puckering with laughter.

Mo sipped her tea. 'Chalk and cheese, then, the son and the daughter.'

'You can say that again! That Eva's a prim sort of madam. Works in a library so I heard and never had a boyfriend till last Christmas. That mum of hers keeps a tight rein, I bet. Renton was lucky to get away from here and with all that family dosh in the offing he's no fool keeping in with his dad.'

'Renny got on well with Suzie.'

'Sure. Why not?'

The sound of a car stopping outside put paid to all this

girly chat and the door burst open to admit Tracey's lover boy, Bill Wickham.

Mo pushed her mug aside and introduced herself. Wickham frowned, his face obdurate.

'I thought I'd seen the last of the fucking police today,' he said, rounding the littered table to reach for a bottle of whisky on the dresser. He poured a stiff tot into one of the dirty mugs and slumped into a chair. 'More questions?' he snapped.

'If you wouldn't mind going over the story one more time, sir.'

Bill Wickham sighed and rattled off his spiel, an exhausted reprise of the finding of the body, his own movements the night before and a terse account of the exact nature of his work.

'Farm manager?' Prentice quoted from her notes.

'Not much of a farm, the fields are mostly rented out. Just a few sheep, more for the look of the thing, the view from the house, if you ask me. The horses are more important. Valuable beasts, touchy bastards, need careful handling. Tracey here's got a soft way with them, a natural horse-whisperer.'

Prentice listened to a glossy amplification of his role at the Grange and got the impression that Wickham, despite his surly manner, was a competent manager and a man with a sense of loyalty.

'Lady Brigham was a fine horsewoman, I heard,' Mo said, watching his reaction with sly interest.

'Fair enough. Not an eventer like Eva but a decent employer.'

'You had no quarrel with Lady B.'

'Suzie? Never a cross word. Suzie was great. If you mean the first Lady Brigham, I'd have to watch my p's and q's.'

'You worked here before Sir William remarried?'

'Been here six years. Eva introduced me, head-hunted me you could say,' he said with a lift of the head, 'from a stud farm in Ireland Sir William has an interest in.'

Prentice closed her notebook and glanced at her watch. 'You will be here all evening, Mr Wickham? My boss, Superintendent Hayes, might like a word.'

He topped up his mug, his mouth hardening. 'What is it with you people? I found the body, OK? End of story.'

'Tracey mentioned that you were unconvinced it was an accident. You touched the body?'

He drew back, taking his time lighting a cigarette.

'Course not. But any fool could see she'd been pushed.'

'Pushed?'

'Suzie wasn't the sort to fall down the stairs, even in the dark.'

'In the dark? No lights on, then?'

He grew impatient and tossed off the whisky. 'How in blazes would I know? By the time I got there it was practically mid-morning – seeing a naked body sprawled out on the bloody floor like fish on a slab was enough to take in, there was no need for me to worry about putting the lights out.'

Mo closed her notebook and stepped towards the door, throwing a warm smile towards Tracey before striding off. Darkness had fallen and all the windows in the big house blazed with light.

She was unsure what to make of Bill Wickham. A handsome bloke if you liked a bit of rough, and exuding undeniable sex appeal. A niggling doubt flickered at the back of her mind, but, she had to admit, horsey types never rang any bells for her. And the brainy guys she fancied seemed generally to turn out to be short-arsed, worse luck.

Six

When Mo Prentice got back to the big house the flurry of excitement had fizzled out and the place was unnaturally silent. Two constables stamped about in the shrubbery and a squad car stood parked across the drive but an atmosphere of abandonment lent a spooky air.

She called out, 'Hello? Anyone at home?'

DI Clarke's sergeant appeared at the top of the stairs. 'Yeah? Oh, it's you. Your boss has followed the mortuary van, wanted to speak to the pathologist before the body's cleaned up.' He jogged downstairs to join her in the hall and Mo noted his mud-caked suede loafers, guessing that she was not the only one to be dragged in off the street on this.

She frowned. 'He took the car?'

'Drove off with the DI, said he'd come back for you later.'

Prentice cursed, wishing Hayes would remember she was in the team, not some unnecessary appendage. What was she supposed to do? Cool her heels here until he deigned to pick her up? She glanced at her watch. It was nearly seven and they hadn't even booked any digs yet.

The sergeant grinned. 'Left you in the lurch, eh? Like to look round the rest of the house while you're waiting?'

Mollified, she followed him upstairs and into the master bedroom, which looked for all the world as if it had been trashed. Hedgecoe put on all the lights, a crystal chandelier with far too many watts giving the room a sharp brilliance. It was like a stage set. But the four-poster with its flesh-coloured brocade hangings was seriously unmade, the silk coverlet tossed on the floor, everything else stripped.

'What happened to the sheets?' she said.

'SOCO bagged them up with the pillows and some under-
wear and stuff.'

She frowned but decided to let it go, anxious not to make
it too obvious that this was her first murder investigation.
She gazed around, admiring the faded grandeur of what
could only be described as a boudoir. An embroidered shawl
lay draped over a chaise-longue under the window but a
French bureau had been crudely emptied, each of its minia-
ture drawers upended. A full-length free-standing mirror
was spotlit like that of a star's dressing room, and the glass
surface of a dressing table was strewn with make-up jars
and clouded by a fine film of talc.

Mo turned to face Hedgecoe. 'Coke?'

He grinned. 'Fingerprinting stuff. Seen enough?'

'SOCO really have cleared out? Anything interesting I
missed?'

He paused, unsure how far the DI wanted to go on this
fact-sharing lark, the official line being that the Sussex force
had requested assistance from the Met in order to retain
objectivity, which to Hedgecoe's mind beggared belief.

Prentice persisted. 'Oh, go on. I'll get a full report later
anyhow.'

'Coke.'

Her eyes narrowed. 'You're having me on.'

'No. Straight up. Found it myself. Just a few grams in a
screw of paper tucked inside a copy of *Horse & Hound* in
that bedside cabinet.'

Prentice stepped round the bed to peer into the gaping
drawer, the remaining contents now neatly stacked on top
with her alarm clock set for six in the morning. No more
early calls for Lady B., then. Poor cow. What a way to
go . . . She was about to steer Sergeant Hedgecoe on with
the conducted tour when her mobile shrilled. It was Hayes.

'I'm at the Red Lion in the village, Prentice. You can
walk it – it's only down the road. I've booked two rooms
and supper at eight. Any fresh evidence from that girl in
the staff cottage? No, never mind. Leave it till later and
we'll put our notes together over a beer. OK?'

Without waiting for a response, he broke off, leaving the

girl in something of a quandary. Hayes' tone had been friendly enough but she was still unsure of her role in all this. With the local boys firmly in charge of the investigation, the arrival of Met officers must present problems, not helped by the seniority of Detective Superintendent Roger Hayes.

She smiled at her reluctant informant. 'I'm staying at the Red Lion, apparently. Any chance of a lift?'

The Red Lion was well outside the village and more of a gastro pub than a scruffy local. The bar was scrupulously free of smokers, the only early evening punters an elderly bar fly wearing a Barbour and two City types in suits. Mo cheerfully greeted the girl refilling the old guy's tankard and four pairs of eyes swivelled to take in the newcomer.

'Hey, you must be Mr Hayes' date,' the barmaid laughingly greeted her. Mo stiffened. 'It's OK – he booked two singles,' she added, winking at the gentleman-farmer lookalike crouched over his beer. Flodde, despite the gentrified aura of a rural beauty spot, was, Mo decided, nothing more than a commuter village, less than an hour's train ride from the big city and providing some very expensive properties for the huntin' and fishin' set. 'Mr Hayes is through there, miss. In the office at the back,' she said, nodding towards a door marked 'Private'.

Hayes sat before a log fire, his feet propped up on the club fender, his head wreathed in cigarette smoke.

'You managed to escape the smoke-free zone, then, sir,' she archly commented, throwing off her jacket and glancing round the licensee's back room.

'Only bloody place,' he cheerfully retorted. 'Here, sit yourself down, Prentice, I got you a Chardonnay, OK?'

She pulled a leather chair closer to the fire and declined the glass with an apologetic shrug. 'Actually, sir, I don't drink.'

He frowned. 'Really? Ah, well that's interesting. A cigarette, then?'

She grinned. 'You know very well I don't smoke, sir. And what's all this about me being your date for tonight?'

'Who said that?'

'The girl serving in the bar.'

'Lizzie? Oh, well, that was a little subterfuge the land-lord and I thought a sensible idea. Some TV people arrived in the village this afternoon and I explained it was neces-sary for us two Met officers to keep our heads down while the local boys were handling the investigation. He kindly offered the use of his office.'

'Oh, right.'

'Something else to drink, Prentice?'

'Ginger ale will do – I'll shout through to the bar, shall I?'

She hurried out and, glancing at the menu while the girl poured her drink, was impressed by the fare on offer.

'Crikey! Just as well my boss is on expenses.'

'Your boss?'

Mo grabbed the glass and turned to go. 'Yeah, Mr Hayes. Likes to think he's a real swinger, know what I mean? Put this on his tab will you, Lizzie? Thanks.'

She grinned as she returned to her seat by the fire. If Hayes had ideas about this teamwork, it would be on her own terms.

Seven

'OK. First up: what did the farm manager's girlfriend have to say?'

Mo removed her jacket and rummaged in her backpack for the notebook. She riffled through the pages and looked up with a smile. 'Actually, not a lot, sir. She liked the victim, reckons she was popular with everyone in the village. Not so enthusiastic about the first Lady Brigham, though, who moved nearby, which must have been an embarrassment for her ex and a supreme irritation for her successor.'

'You got the address?'

'Er, no, not yet, sir, but Tracey Wilson's lived in Flodde all her life so she's well acquainted with all the local gossip.'

'Did she tell you about the row the ex-Lady B. had with the deceased in the local post office?' Mo shook her head. 'Well, ask around, Prentice. Find out what it was all about. I'm surprised the kid didn't mention it.'

'We were interrupted by her boyfriend returning from a lengthy shake-down at the nick.'

'Wickham?'

'That's the guy. Moody at first but a long-standing employee transferred from the stud farm Sir William has in Ireland. Brought over to look after his horses here. Says he's not just the stable manager but runs the entire estate – some of the fields are rented out to local farmers and presumably Sir William has a regular place in London.'

'Notting Hill. The Grange is just a weekend home.'

'But his wife spent a lot of time here, sir. According to Tracey she was often here alone when Sir William was abroad but funnily enough she booted Mrs Cosham, the housekeeper, out of her estate cottage because "she didn't like staff living in". A lonely place like the Grange could be a target for burglars, why choose to be home alone? – I don't suppose he was on any terrorist hit list, was he, sir? The Commander would have warned us.'

Hayes shook his head. 'More likely our victim suspected the housekeeper was a snitch. Carrying tales to the first Lady B. about the new young wifelet. Liked her privacy, eh? Well, why not? I want to see this housekeeper woman. If our Suzie had been attacked on any other night it would have been Mrs Cosham who found the body first thing Thursday morning instead of Wickham. Convenient being off stage. For all we know she gave the tip-off to the attacker that the lady would be in the house on her own. Apparently, this Mrs Cosham has Tuesdays and Thursdays off so she can work through the weekend, which is when the family are normally here and when guests are entertained.'

'Tracey has some sort of regular job at the big house helping the housekeeper.'

'What did you make of the girl? Honest?'

'Nice kid, too young to be shacked up with Wickham I'd say, and from what she said, her mum hates the guy.'

'The family's local?'

'The mother and two brothers live in a caravan in the village.'

'Gyppos?'

'No! Homeless after being chucked out of their council house owing to persistent rent arrears.'

'No man on the scene?'

'Seems not. Would it be useful if I went to see Mrs Wilson, Tracey's mum? Get the low-down on Wickham?'

Hayes sipped his beer and eyed his sergeant with interest. Maybe she wasn't such a hindrance after all, though he'd have to curb this 'bull in a china shop' approach of hers. 'Yeah, maybe . . . I'll have a go at the housekeeper and you can talk to the postmistress and find out what the row was all about. The two Lady Brighams head-to-head must have gone the rounds in the village.'

A knock at the door broke up this line of thought. It was the pub landlord.

'Supper's being served, sir. Would you and the young lady like to sit down now or see your rooms first?'

Mo jumped up. 'I need to clean up and fetch my bag from the car.'

Hayes rose and handed over the keys, his head brushing the low beams. 'Lead on, Ted, I'll wait for my colleague in the dining room.'

Mo strode off to the car and the landlord showed Hayes to a corner table in a room already half filled with a chattering crowd. He glanced round. Locals, at a guess: well-upholstered residents from the gin-and-Jaguar belt, luckily. Not a scruffy reporter in sight.

Hayes refused to discuss the case over dinner, anxious not to draw the attention of the couple at the next table. The menu offered a fare well above the scratch meals he had become used to since moving to his studio flat in Wapping. But there had to be some compensations for a job change that had, so far, been no dream ticket as described by Commander Crick. Renting a pad on the top floor of a converted warehouse overlooking the river was a stopgap, underlining a reluctance to admit that the change of scene was permanent. On good days he found himself veering towards estate agents' windows but the commitment of putting his life in hock to a mortgage set his pulse racing. He'd been down that road before and it had been rocky.

After coffee he suggested they return to the Grange for a last look round. 'Clarke has set up an incident room in the estate office. I've got some unanswered questions.'

They parked on the drive and approached the panda car where two 'uniforms' were relaxing all too well. One sprang out to salute the superintendent, the intervention of Met officers on the case being a touchy subject.

Hayes flashed his ID. 'Anyone on duty, Constable?'

'Sergeant Hedgecoe's packing up the paperwork, sir. He's in the incident room. Shall I direct you?'

'Round the back of the stables? No problem.'

Hayes headed off at a trot with Mo in his wake to track down Hedgecoe. They found him sorting what looked like rent ledgers and telephone accounts on a trestle table where a pretty WPC was working at a newly installed computer.

'Still hard at it, Sergeant? No let-up, then.'

'DI Clarke's just left, sir. He tried to phone you at the pub but you'd already left.'

'Any developments?'

'Skid marks in the mud off at the side of the drive. It looks like a quick getaway, the driver reversed into a tree leaving flakes of red car paint that were bagged up and are being tested. The boys are checking but someone left sharpish after the rain on Wednesday night.'

'No witnesses?'

'Not so far, sir.'

'Any joy with the phone records?'

'Still checking, sir.'

Hayes grew exasperated, peeved by the invidious situation he was in, neither in charge of the bloody investigation nor in a situation which allowed him to pull rank. Mo stepped back, throwing a weak smile at the girl at the computer who, mesmerized by the clear irritation of the senior officer, mentally applauded Hedgecoe's stone-walling. Some cool dude. Maybe she would take him up on that offer of a drink later after all.

Hayes turned on his heel and headed back to the car, Mo once more finding herself in tow like a lolloping bridesmaid at a shotgun wedding.

Back at the Red Lion they repaired to the landlord's office and Hayes persuaded Ted to allow an after-hours nightcap.

Mo slumped in a chair by the ashes of the log fire. 'We don't seem to be in the loop on this one, sir.'

'You're bloody right, Prentice. Why don't we call it a day and get to grips with this Brigham murder in the morning? I've been invited to attend the autopsy.'

Eight

Hayes left Mo in the village and drove to the mortuary. DI Clarke was called from the lab and met him in the narrow corridor leading from the pathologist's sanguineous arena. Hayes drew a sharp breath, the stench of death striking him like a blow.

'Red Lion OK, sir?'

'Very comfortable, thank you, Inspector. Let's hope we can clear up this case quickly, the media are scenting blood. I gather that suspicious tyre marks found in the grounds are under review?'

'Plaster casts are ready now, sir, and first impression is of a sports car not instantly linked to the local scene but worth keeping in mind. There was one peculiarity our mechanic got excited about – one odd tyre, brand new, the others well worn, a dangerous combination and suggesting an owner not too fussy with maintenance.'

They hurried into the lab where the pathologist, introduced to Hayes as Doctor Harris, was already examining Suzie Brigham's brain tissue. Another genial type, Hayes noted, a characteristic he had frequently come across in the pathology line of business. Gory work but perhaps the absence of any call to effect any medical cure was a comfort; no complaints from the dead, no recriminations regarding any misdiagnosis. Hayes shrugged off a curious line of thought and waited for Doctor Harris to complete this delicate stage of the post-mortem.

'The young woman died after an initial heavy blow to the left side of the head that split the scalp, broke open the skull and entered the brain. As I see it, the attack came from behind, a left-handed man I'd say. The victim would have died almost instantaneously although secondary wounds would indicate the assailant continued to rain blows after the deceased fell. There are minor injuries consistent with a subsequent fall – she was found at the bottom of the stairs, I understand?'

'Yes, Doctor, but a jet of blood sprayed against the wainscot halfway up would indicate that the lady was first attacked while she was fleeing either up or down. A shoe dropped at that point but it's difficult to draw any firm conclusion,' Clarke added.

'No defence wounds, Inspector, no sign of a struggle, but a series of strong blows inflicted with accuracy even if the woman *was* attempting to get back to the landing. Found naked, you said? Disturbed in bed by noises below and the killer chased her back upstairs?'

Clarke threw a questioning look at Hayes, who appeared to be unimpressed by the suggestions batting forth between the two men.

'Is the primary wound consistent with the suggested weapon?'

'The shillelagh?' The pathologist laughed. 'A first for me, my boy, but my assistant tested skull fragments adhering to this cudgel and there's no mistake about it. Interesting . . .'

'Blood type?'

'That of the victim.' He paused. 'There is one other important point, gentlemen. Our unfortunate lady was approximately four months pregnant. And she had sexual intercourse just prior to her death.'

Clarke drew back, visibly shaken. 'Rape?'

'No bruises, no signs of force. An agreeable pairing, I'd say.'

'Any DNA samples, Doctor Harris?' Hayes broke in, excitement tingling his scalp like static.

Harris focused on the Met officer he had been warned about. 'Of course, Superintendent. Standard procedure. Tests are already in hand.'

'This sexual encounter may have nothing to do with the attack,' Clarke countered, 'the break-in that night being a coincidence.'

'But there *was* no break-in, was there?' Hayes insisted. 'You're not suggesting Lady Brigham let the interloper in herself?'

'It's a possibility, Clarke. Unlikely, I grant you, but not something we can discount. Perhaps a window was left open? A door unlocked?' He glanced at the pathologist and the figure in the green gown and blood-spattered apron stared back, his features etched starkly under the brilliant lights suspended from the ceiling.

Hayes turned to the DI, failing to curb his impatience. 'Doctor Harris, from his experience, puts forward the theory that the woman was disturbed in the bedroom and was halfway downstairs when she was attacked.'

The pathologist grew impatient now. 'Excuse me, but may I suggest you continue your deliberations elsewhere? I have work to do.'

Clarke and Hayes subsided into abject silence and watched the pathologist finish up. The smell of formalin and sterilizing liquid hung over them like a pall and Hayes forced himself to examine the pale corpse with professional detachment.

The waxy complexion seemed slack, the sagging breasts almost deflated, a different creature entirely from the body he had observed at the crime scene. The skin now appeared greyish, the skull sawn open and plundered, the livid lines of the scalpel's entry violating the slender torso, the beauty of a girl now reduced to meat on a slab. Hayes turned away and left Clarke to it. He had seen enough.

Mo spent the morning pacing the village, finding her bearings. Not that there was much to see, the Red Lion being at least a mile beyond the huddle of cottages round the duck pond, the church even further outside the centre and Aspern Grange standing well clear of the hoi polloi.

The post office and general store occupied a key position and looked as if it supplied all basic needs.

She strolled inside and surveyed the stock: milk, bread, vegetables and a substantial freezer cabinet, not to mention cigarettes, wine and cans of beer. A sandwich and a Coke seemed a good intro, and while passing over the cash she made a stab at casual chit-chat with the gorgon behind the till. But if Linda Foote was indeed the owner whose name appeared on the notice over the door, the person licensed to sell the hard stuff, she was having none of Mo's bonhomie. Probably thinks I'm one of the press hacks who's moved into the village, asking rude questions about the deceased lady of the manor. Mo gave up and produced her warrant card.

'Mrs Foote. I wonder if you were a witness to an argument in here recently between the Brigham ladies?'

'No.'

'You're sure? I've been reliably informed that there was a full-blooded row and this is a small establishment, difficult to talk in private.'

'I don't eavesdrop, Sergeant, and I don't gossip. I wouldn't last the month in this village if I tittle-tattled.'

'Yes, but this is a murder enquiry, Mrs Foote.'

'Sorry. I don't know what you're talking about and I'd like you to leave my shop now, please.'

Mo battled on but the postmistress blanked her out, denying all knowledge of any such encounter on her premises. Mo persisted. No joy. And after several fruitless approaches with diminishing effect, she departed with nothing but a scratch lunch. She wondered if her experience of questioning businessmen at the Serious Fraud Office had permanently skewed her interviewing technique and decided to try her luck with Tracey's mum.

The caravan was parked behind the smithy as Tracey had described but no one was at home, not even the boys. At school? It really wasn't her day, was it?

She returned to her room at the Red Lion and phoned the office and appealed to Maurice Gibson, the forty-six-year-old IT specialist with a kind heart.

'Mo? How's it going? You sound depressed.'

'Not much headway so far, Morry, and, frankly, I'm feeling out of my depth.'

'Hayes being difficult?'

'Not familiar with team games that one, but, to be fair, I'm new to murder, fraudsters being more in my line.'

'Anything I can do?'

'I was wondering if you could do a recce for me? This bloke, Sir William Brigham, chucked in a gold-plated job as Chief Executive at Bluetex Pharmaceuticals to take a serious dip in salary to work in Brussels.'

'Well, he did get a knighthood out of it.'

'Yeah, but, seriously, Morry, it sounds funny to me.'

'Like you said, Mo, you're used to fraudsters with only an eye for the moolah. Maybe Brigham got the call? Good works? An urge for a socially acceptable career change?'

'Is Bluetex dodgy?'

'Brigham was the finance guy, but who knows, he might have had a burst of conscience, decided to hand in his ritzy lifestyle and concentrate on his horses.'

'A serious change of heart? What about the new wife?'

Maurice Gibson chuckled. He liked Mo and was as much at sea with this new intelligence unit as the rest of the team. 'The new wife came later, there's still the first Lady Brigham out there somewhere. Come now, what's really bothering you, Mo?'

'The file we got from Bennet's awfully thin. Could you trawl through your own channels and send me a fuller biography? And anything you can dig up about the ex-wife and the children – a daughter, Eva, and a son, I forget his name, but both in their late twenties or early thirties at a guess.'

'Righto. Leave it with me. Email still kosher? We're not treading on Hayes' toes with this, are we?'

Mo crossed her fingers. 'Course not, Morry. Thanks a bunch.'

Nine

Hayes phoned Mo and told her to make her way to the housekeeper's address.

'Where's that, sir?'

'Bluebell Cottage. Next to a pub called the George. Ten minutes.'

'You're joking! It's a good mile from here and I've no wheels.'

He laughed. 'Healthy girl like you? Eight minutes max.'

Bluebell Cottage stood behind a picket fence and a neatly barbered privet, the garden still bravely glowing with ragged red and yellow dahlias. Mo arrived red-faced and breathless just as Hayes was ringing the doorbell. A large woman in a flowery apron opened the door, her grey hair crimped like a 1930s ad for a Marcel wave, her eyes etched with laughter lines.

'Mrs Cosham?' Hayes cheerfully enquired, brandishing his warrant card and nudging Mo to flash her ID.

'No, I'm May. Cissie's out back taking down the runner beans. You must be here about that poor Lady Brigham, I shouldn't wonder.' She led them through to the sitting room and opened a window. 'Cissie! Two nice policemen to see you, dear.'

Hayes and Mo Prentice stood to attention in a room gilded with autumn sunshine, a room crowded with too many chairs, and little tables crammed with knick-knacks.

The stout party in the apron closed the window and gently lifted a cat from the sofa. 'Sit down, love,' she said, squeezing Mo's elbow, 'you look proper flushed. I seen you rushing round the village all morning, you poor soul.'

A sharp voice issued from the back door. 'Nothing goes unnoticed in Flodde if my sister's behind the net curtains.' A scrawny version of May appeared from the kitchen, wiping her hands on a towel before footing the displaced moggy outside.

'Mrs Cosham?' Hayes repeated, wondering how two such diverse offspring could share the same genes. The late Suzie Brigham's housekeeper wore a pleated skirt and a blue twin-set, her hair as severely styled as her sister's, but there the similarity ended. 'And what can I do for you?' she said, giving Hayes her full attention.

'I'm Detective Superintendent Hayes and this is my sergeant. I have some questions about your work at the Grange. Please make yourself comfortable.'

Ignoring this, she remained standing. 'I've already told Inspector Clarke all I know. I don't live in and I am not required on Thursdays.'

Mo took out her notebook and waited for Hayes to continue. It looked as if questioning Cissie Cosham would be akin to pulling teeth.

Unabashed, Hayes returned the woman's unblinking gaze, noting her tightly clasped hands, the sole indication of any tension.

'Bear with me, Mrs Cosham, I like to get the story from the horse's mouth.' Mo bit her lip, wishing that Hayes had chosen another metaphor.

'Am I correct,' he continued, 'in assuming you moved out of the staff cottage two years ago?'

Her mouth tightened. 'Indeed so. My sister here, Miss Cripps, kindly took me in.'

'There was a problem at the big house? A disagreement? Criticism of the extent of your duties?'

'Absolutely not! My work was never in question. Lady Brigham,' she said stiffly, 'insisted she needed my cottage for a new stable girl, though, in all this time,' she added bitterly, 'no new staff have been employed. And I've got more than enough to do with only that silly girl, Tracey, to help.'

'No one else lives in?'

'Bill Wickham has his own place and the gardener's part time. It's the horses take first place up there, believe you me.'

'Only three, if I'm reliably informed.'

'She was always on to Sir William to buy more, God knows why, it's not as if Wickham can decently exercise the ones they've got once Miss Eva left home. Even that useless Tracey gets to ride and the jumps have never been used since that terrible accident.'

'Accident?'

'When young Rosie Kipling got killed – didn't you know that?'

Hayes' eyes glinted. 'I'm a stranger here. Tell me, Mrs Cosham. A riding accident at the Grange?'

'The new milady,' she spat out, 'killed that poor child, if the truth be known.'

'Oh, Cissie! You can't believe that.'

Cosham rounded on her sister, eyes blazing. 'Everyone in the village thought so, May, and if it hadn't been for that coroner turning a blind eye Suzie Brigham would have been locked up. Sir William got her off, I swear he did. Old-boy stuff with that coroner and—'

'Excuse me here, Mrs Cosham. Rosie Kipling?'

'Two summers ago, just before I came here to live with May. Rosie was Lennie Kipling's eldest. Only fifteen and horse-mad like all the girls her age. Wickham and milady set up this club, see, for the local kids, bought in four ponies and gave free lessons in exchange for cleaning out the stables. Trouble was, that flighty madam didn't do it properly, did she? Tried to run it all her own way, wouldn't even take Bill Wickham's warnings. It was a tragedy waiting to happen – the fences were too high, the girth was too tight making the poor bloody horse frisky and that poor child came off head first and broke her neck. Died on the spot.'

'No hard hat?'

'Fat difference that made!'

'But Lady Brigham was exonerated?'

Cissie Cosham's mouth trembled and May half rose, then fell back, knowing the futility of it all.

'Lennie Kipling was Sir William's mole-catcher and handyman before all this happened. Went berserk he did, and bashed Bill Wickham over the head with a bottle when they was in the George one Saturday night. Lost his job and got six months for it, the stupid beggar. Been on the dole ever since and his poor wife with three other kids to bring up. It wasn't Bill's fault and Lennie knew it, but the man just *had* to hit out at someone and he hasn't been allowed to set foot on the estate since Rosie died.'

'The ponies were sold,' May whispered.

Hayes coughed, raising an eyebrow at Mo before excusing himself. 'I seem to have distressed you, Mrs Cosham. Perhaps we should continue this tomorrow. Meet me at the estate office at ten. I have questions about your relationship with Lady Brigham.'

'The *real* Lady Brigham,' she said meaningfully.

'The *late* Lady Brigham. I shall be speaking to the former Lady Brigham in my own good time.'

Mo edged to the door, smiling weakly at May Cripps, who looked tearful. 'Thank you – we can see ourselves out,' she murmured.

Hayes was grimly silent as he drove them back to the Red Lion. It was only as they entered the lounge bar that he pulled her aside. 'Print all that for me, will you, Prentice? And see if you can find out if this bloke Kipling's still in the district. And you'd better get back to Tracey and ask her about the accident. I thought she told you "everyone in the village liked Suzie"? Cosham's version doesn't support that if she's not just bitching since she lost her cottage. And Bill Wickham's kept very quiet about it – a child's death on the estate must have been a major scandal at the time, especially if Wickham was blamed by the kid's father. Search out the press cuttings and have another go at Tracey's mum – maybe she took Kipling's side and having her daughter shacked up with Wickham's too much to swallow.'

'If Mrs Cosham was moody with the Brighams after the accident no wonder Suzie wanted her out.'

'Sir William would find it difficult to justify dismissing

a long-term employee like Cosham on those grounds and probably hoped to keep in with the villagers. Getting the housekeeper out of the staff cottage would probably be enough to pacify Suzie without his being sued for unfair dismissal if he got shot of the woman altogether, and I wouldn't mind betting she got a lump sum in compensation, enough to set her up in another place of her own.'

'Can't say I'd like to have her cooking *my* dinner if I was Suzie, and Mrs Cosham had openly spoken out after the Kipling accident.'

'We must ask the ex-Lady Brigham what she thought of her as a housekeeper. Do we know how long she worked for the family?'

Mo shook her head.

Hayes shrugged. 'Well, Cosham's not important at this stage. Get on to Hedgecoe. I've got some phone calls to make but ask if the landlord could drum up some sandwiches and coffee for us in his office. I missed lunch. We can go over today's work and you can tell me what you've been up to getting yourself "proper flushed", as May Cripps put it.'

Ten

Leaving his sergeant to type up the notes, Hayes drove to the temporary incident room set up in the estate-office block to seek out Detective Inspector Clarke. Feeling himself something of an unknown quantity on this investigation, the necessity to keep in with the local guys was irksome if unavoidable.

Hayes was no good at all this polite tap-dancing stuff, his natural abrasive style sitting ill with the diplomatic mission Bennet seemed to think was necessary. In truth, Hayes was curious about this bloke Brigham, some sort of minor VIP yet able to demand the protection of two Met officers. The murder had the markings of a local crime and the Sussex CID with all their background info were more than capable of sorting it out without any interference from London.

Did Sir William have something to hide? Chucking a top job for a stint in Brussels, for instance? Was there some murky subtext there, something important enough to involve Commander Crick's new security unit headed by an officer with no experience of such work but a whole bagful of dirty murder cases on his CV?

On reflection Hayes had to admit that he'd been wrong about one thing: Sergeant Morwenna Prentice. She had, despite his misgivings, turned out to be useful, although working with a new sidekick was never going to be easy. She had a certain way with her which at first was hard to pinpoint; slightly gauche and not a girl to flaunt her feminine charms but attractive in an offbeat way, and quietly determined. Determined. He'd have to watch that, keep her on a short rein or she'd be off at a gallop.

Hayes smiled at this uncharacteristic horsey line of thought. All that talk about Suzie Brigham's riding skills was affecting his concentration. Trouble was, even if Sir William was unaware of it, 'riding' was probably the thing Suzie was best at, even if it was between the matrimonial sheets while he was pontificating in Europe. The poor sod. Did he know what he was taking on when he ditched his long-time wife for such a lively filly?

He was lucky to find DI Clarke in. The man was clearly up to his eyes with the case, probably the most high-profile investigation of his career. The media had latched on to it, though the details of the attack were still under wraps. But already Suzie's pals had been persuaded to join up the dots and even her ex-husband, Fritz Grice, had put in a good word for her.

Apart from her disaffected housekeeper, Suzie Brigham seemed to have made few enemies. A real charmer, it was generally agreed. Beautiful, generous with local charities, approachable and popular even with her former girl friends on the catwalk, models who apparently harboured no ill feelings towards the lucky girl who had passed seamlessly from a first marriage to a top photographer to a gilded future with a wealthy man old enough to be her uncle.

Trevor Clarke had set himself up at Wickham's desk in the requisitioned estate-management block. The office comprised two interconnecting rooms and a kitchen, the outer room a secretarial annexe fitted with computers and a bank of filing cabinets and buzzing with activity. The inner sanctum was sparsely furnished, the walls hung with certificates, photographs from the parade ring and winners' rosettes.

The DI looked up as Hayes appeared, and beckoned him inside. Hayes pulled up a chair, dumped his flimsy leather document case on the desk and smiled. 'Any developments, Inspector?'

'Not so far, sir. Any joy at your end? I hear your sergeant's been putting herself round the village.'

'She mentioned some interesting items which you must

already know about but were news to me. The business of a fight between Bill Wickham and a bloke called Kipling.'

'Oh, that was two years ago. Quite out of character, according to the local bobby.'

'Kipling's daughter died after a riding accident at the Grange. Nasty stuff.'

'That's right. But you're not thinking Kipling still had it in for Lady B. over that, are you, sir? Two years on?'

Hayes shrugged. 'Unlikely, but he's obviously a man with a serious grudge. His daughter's death, according to Mrs Cosham, was Suzie Brigham's fault. Gross negligence – a lack of supervision of a young girl inexperienced in competitive jumping?'

'Lady Brigham was entirely exonerated. Wickham swore that Rosie saddled up the horse herself and the coroner accepted his word.'

'Well, even so, have you checked Kipling's movements on Wednesday night?'

Clarke drew back. 'Not yet, sir, but we're getting to it. Bit short-handed, to tell the truth. Did your sergeant think there's more to it? Fresh evidence? A new witness?'

'No, but so far we've no other lead, have we?'

Clarke shook his head. 'Kipling's not the killer – she'd never have let him in for a start, especially late at night.'

'Well, there *was* a man in her bed that night, the pathologist has his bloody DNA. Let's hope we don't end up having to test every red-blooded male in the village. We could start with Wickham.'

'You're convinced it's a local killer, Superintendent?'

'Not *convinced*. Logically a girl like Suzie would have no truck with the peasantry. But some women like a bit of rough for a change.'

Clarke grinned. 'If you say so, sir.'

'No gossip about gentleman callers?' Hayes sarcastically retorted.

'None.'

'Any sighting of a car?'

'Not yet, sir, but my mechanic seems to think the tyre tracks were from an old MG Sports.'

'Really? Hardly the sort of banger to belong to a rich contender for Suzie's affections, I'd have thought. Keep working on it, man. What's your take on Wickham?'

'As a suspect? Well, he's got a way with the girls, apparently. All that Irish blarney. And he's as keen on the nags as the victim was, but in bed with the boss's wife?' He shook his head. 'More'n his job's worth and he's been with Sir William for a good many years, worked for that stud farm in Ireland since he was a stable lad so I hear. And Tracey would have noticed him sniffing round the big house.'

'His alibi stands up?'

'In the George till closing time and straight home.'

'Tracey clocked him in?'

Clarke nodded.

'And the pub landlord backs him up?'

'It was darts night. Busy.'

'He can't vouch for Wickham being there all evening?'

Clarke chewed his lip. 'Not on oath – the place was packed out.'

Hayes slumped in his seat and gave Clarke a searching look. 'OK. The village stuff's all yours – I'm here to look after Sir William's interests. Have you spoken to him about the pathologist's findings?'

'Superintendent Fox is a tactful man but—'

'Brigham's reaction?'

'He's a po-faced bugger – excuse my French. But frankly, Mr Hayes, the situation was a minefield, what with his ex Zita chewing his head off every time he appeared in the village and that girl of theirs stoking the flames. Though,' he quietly added, 'things have perked up between her and her dad since the boyfriend came on the scene.'

'Eh?'

'Eva got herself a fiancé – it was in all the quality papers. "The engagement is announced between Miss Eva Maria Brigham of Aspern Grange, Flodde, and . . ." I forget his name. There was a big party at the house in the summer, pictures all over the local rag, biggest spread all year. A bloody miracle. Talk was she must be a lezzie, no boyfriends ever, and suddenly up pops this bloke and, hey presto, he's bought the ring and set about buying an antiques business in Horsham.'

'What's the matter with her, then?'

Clarke opened his hands in mock dismay. 'Nothing. Clever, not a bad looker, terrific horsewoman but firmly under Zita's thumb. Poor kid never stood a chance, the only escape was when she got herself a job and Sir William bought her a flat in London.'

Hayes raised a hand. 'Well, let's concentrate on the essentials, shall we? I have to talk to Sir William – OK with you and Superintendent Fox? Is he staying at the Grange?'

'Can't stand the place, and who can blame him? The son, Renton, accompanied him to the mortuary and afterwards they went straight back to the London house.'

'Elgin Mews.'

Clarke nodded.

'Then I'll shoot off there in the morning after I've interviewed Mrs Cosham here at ten. You won't need this office for an hour or so? I thought I'd get more out of her here than down at the station. Recording equipment installed?'

'Top class. Will you need a typist?'

'No, Sergeant Prentice will be on hand. Have you spoken to this bloody-minded housekeeper yet?'

Clarke gave a wry grin. 'Hedgecoe had that pleasure. Mrs Cosham never got over being shunted off the estate. It made her bitter.'

'Bitter enough to bash our Suzie over the head?'

Eleven

Cissie Cosham arrived on the dot of ten, leaned her bike against the wall and left her wet cycle cape to drip onto the quarry-tiled floor of the outer office.

Mo hurried over. 'Goodness, Mrs Cosham, you're wet through. Can I bring you a cup of tea? The Superintendent's waiting in here for you.'

'In Wickham's room?'

'That's right. We're using his office for the time being.'

Suzie's housekeeper was not going to be mollified by any cup of tea, and strode into the back room without a backward glance, leaving Mo to follow.

Hayes hastily rose and waited for the women to seat themselves. 'Nice of you to be so punctual, Mrs Cosham.'

'I'm still waiting to be allowed back to the house – there must be a lot of mess to clear up and Sir William likes everything spick and span.'

Hayes ignored this and ploughed on. 'Any objection to my recording our little chat?'

'I've got nothing to hide,' she retorted, adjusting her tortoiseshell glasses. She wore a tweed suit and leather boots, an outfit not unbecoming and, in fact, rather expensive-looking. Hayes wondered if Suzie Brigham passed on her cast-offs to the staff but quickly dismissed this as something the woman sitting opposite would doubtless find offensive.

Mo switched on the equipment and murmured, 'Just a convenience, Mrs Cosham, nothing official.'

Hayes frowned, hoping Prentice was not going to put her spoke in whenever she felt like it. He liked to set the tone of interviews himself, liked to pick and choose how to approach witnesses, especially hostile ones, and to his mind Cissie Cosham needed no soft touch.

After an initial skirmish around her hours of work, Hayes dived in, his gaze sharp as a laser. 'Right, now we've covered the basics, can I establish the exact nature of your job and the number of staff involved.'

Cissie relaxed into a whingeing complaint about the lack of domestic help at the Grange which he cut short with a curt nod. 'Yes, I get your drift, Mrs Cosham, but can you be precise? Your main responsibility was in the cooking department, am I right? Lady Brigham gave you a free hand with the menus and ordering of supplies for the house and unless guests were expected or Sir William was home you ran the show?'

'Smooth as silk and never a complaint in all the years I've been here.'

'And how long is that?'

'Twenty-seven years come Christmas.'

Mo looked up sharply, impressed by the woman's composure. Having got into her stride there was now no stopping her.

'Of course, there was more entertaining when Lady Zita was here. Lovely musical evenings we had, very important weekend guests.'

Hayes perked up. 'Musical evenings?'

'Lady Zita was a professional before she married. Sang at the Metropolitan in New York!'

Hayes' face fell. 'Oh, a singer.'

'Soprano.'

'Of course,' he added drily, 'but let's get up to date, shall we, Mrs Cosham? From my notes I understand you had Tracey to help in the house and a gardener who presumably provided vegetables and flowers for the table. I noticed an extensive glasshouse in the walled garden at the back here. Who else?'

She settled back in her chair and counted off each name with a raised finger. 'Beryl Sheldrake helped out in the kitchen preparing vegetables and washing the pots when we had visitors. My sister May did the flower arrangements and laid the tables and a woman from the village came in once a week to deal with the laundry.'

'And her name was?' Mo put in.

'Er, Betty Kipling.'

Hayes raised an eyebrow. 'And who tidied the bedrooms and changed the sheets for Mrs Kipling?'

'Tracey was responsible for the upstairs.'

'And Tracey did the house cleaning?'

Cissie's stern expression dissolved. 'Tracey? No way. I wouldn't trust Tracey to do a thorough job. Good enough at what I call cushion patting and, to be fair, she always left the bedrooms nice and tidy whatever time the guests got up – out to the stables before breakfast some of 'em.'

'Horsey people?'

'Lately, yes.'

'No more musical evenings, then?'

She shrugged, a mulish gloom descending like a thunder cloud. 'Not since Lady Zita left.'

'OK. I get the picture, Mrs Cosham. But you still haven't said who did the regular cleaning.'

'Well, actually, it was a lad. Stevie Marsh, the baker's eldest boy. Sent here from the Job Centre and, after a bit of chivvying, Stevie turned out to be the best cleaner we've ever had. Put some elbow grease into it and made a smashing job of the silver.'

Hayes jotted some figures on his pad and smiled. 'Five apart from the gardener and yourself. Not such a bad staff ratio, I'd say.'

'It's a big house!' she countered. 'And some of 'em's part-time, remember. May and Beryl just help out when Sir William has people staying.'

'Lady Brigham also invited friends for the weekend?'

'No, never. The horsey lot were *his* pals or people from the stud farm in Ireland.'

'Lady Brigham liked her privacy, then? Enjoyed having the place to herself? No London friends, ladies' luncheons even?'

'No, nothing like that.'

'Family?'

'None I ever heard of. Not even when we had that big party for Miss Eva.'

'Her engagement party in the summer.'

She nodded so vehemently even the stiff hairdo shifted several degrees. 'Talk of the county, that do was. Beautiful day and she looked lovely.'

'You've known Miss Brigham since she was a child, of course.'

'Like I said, I've been here twenty-seven years. Seen those two grow up, young Renton and Eva.'

Hayes put down his pen. 'Well, thank you, Mrs Cosham, you've been a great help. Perhaps you'll excuse me – I have an appointment in London this afternoon. Maybe I could get back to you later? My sergeant here will make a note of all the addresses of the staff.'

He switched off the recording machine and she got to her feet, settling her shoulder bag and pushing back the chair. But before she could escape to the outer office with Mo, Hayes put what he hoped sounded like an afterthought. 'Just one more thing, Mrs Cosham. In your opinion, was the second marriage happy?'

She eyed him fiercely, and stood stiffly to attention. 'Far be it for me to comment on my employers' private lives, Superintendent, but I must say it was a sad day when Sir William became infatuated with that woman. Anyone but a blind man could see she would only lead him a merry dance, and I said so straight from the start.'

'You saw her with someone?'

She turned on her heel but paused in the doorway. 'How could I? She made damn sure I was off the premises, didn't she?'

Twelve

After watching Cissie Cosham cycle off in the rain Mo rejoined Hayes and waited for him to conclude a phone call.

'Close the door,' he said, 'and sit down. We shall have to reschedule.'

'Yes, sir.'

'I want you to stay here and follow up some enquiries in the village. Tracey Wilson for a start. The kid's lying. Says Suzie was popular with *everyone*, which she wasn't.'

'Mrs Cosham's no guide, sir. She had an axe to grind, and she's still harking back to the days here before Sir William divorced his first wife.'

'Yeah, sure, but I'm betting the housekeeper wasn't the only one. There was this Kipling guy. Bill Wickham shifted the blame for saddling up the dead girl's horse and it was his testimony that got Suzie off the hook with the coroner. Was it true? Or was Wickham persuaded to put a different slant on the accident? Sir William stayed loyal to the guy and probably pays him generously despite the fact that there are only three nags in the stables – hardly big time compared with the stud-farm set-up in Ireland he was used to.'

'But he supervises the estate too, sir, keeps the accounts and seems to run the place in Sir William's absence. No small responsibility.'

Hayes tossed this aside with a flick of the hand. 'Small beer for an ambitious bloke like Wickham. Get back to Tracey and put her in a chatty mood. See what she knows about Wickham's plans for the future and also sound her out about the fight with this Kipling character. If Mrs Cosham gives Kipling's wife a regular job at the big house, what impression did Tracey get about the woman's take on the fatal accident? I would hardly imagine a mother who still blamed the lady of the house for contributing to her girl's death would want to work for her, would you? Make a date with the coroner's officer and get an unbiased version of the way the inquest went. So far we've only heard village gossip. There's more to it, Prentice, and I'm not the guy to persuade Tracey to loosen up.'

'The laundry is a problem, sir. If Mrs Kipling saw Lady Brigham's sheets every week she'd be the first to discover any "naughties" while Sir William was away.'

'Tracey could be covering up for Suzie – being as she seems to have been her biggest fan.'

Mo looked doubtful. 'Since Kipling lost his job at the Grange he's been on the dole. The family need the money, sir – jobs can't be all that easy to come by for his wife with children still at school.'

'Rubbish! People round here are crying out for cleaners and I bet the supermarket could do with part-time staff, shelf-stackers at the very least. Is this Mrs Kipling dim or something?'

'Well, taking on the weekly wash isn't exactly brain surgery, is it, sir? Frankly, I can't see why the Brighams don't use a laundry service like everyone else.'

'Oh, employing the villagers would be traditional for a bloke like Brigham, who sees himself as the local squire. It probably goes back to the way Zita liked to run things. Cosham's not the sort to change that.'

'Don't you get the feeling that Suzie gave up on making an impression here after the failure of her little pony club? The horses were sold and there must have been talk after Kipling's fight with Wickham in the pub.'

'The other pub, you mean? The George?'

'It's not like the Red Lion, where we're staying, sir. It's not exactly a spit-and-sawdust place, but it seems to cater for the locals, while the Red Lion is more of a gastro pub for the well heeled.'

Hayes looked pensive. 'Mm. Perhaps I should spend an hour or two down there one night. Get the feel of the place.'

Mo giggled. 'Darts night would be best. You any good at darts, sir?'

Hayes glanced at his watch. 'Christ! Look at the time. I've got to go, I've screwed Sir William down to an interview at two and afterwards I need to have a serious conference with the Commander and Superintendent Bennet about our remit. We're working in the dark, Prentice. There's more fluff under the bed with Brigham and we're never going to get to grips with this case till we know the full story.'

'You're meeting Sir William at headquarters?'

'No, at his home. A mews house in Notting Hill. His son, Renton, agreed to meet me there and must have persuaded his father to cooperate. Funny family, eh? Daughter barely on speaking terms with the old guy and the son in his pocket.'

'Not so unusual after a divorce, sir. The daughter sides with her mother but the son sees Suzie as a glamorous new stepmother.'

'More likely the son knows what side his bread's buttered keeping in with Sir William. Got a view on this family feud?'

'The daughter's engagement must have broken the ice. You remember Cosham mentioned that the parents gave a big celebration party at the Grange.'

'Who's the fiancé?'

'No idea.'

'Let's go and see this Lady Zita when I get back. Might be interesting. Get the address from Hedgecoe and make an appointment over the weekend if possible. That way we get to kill two birds with one stone, meet the daughter at the same time.'

'Tracey did say Eva spends most weekends with her mother and since the engagement the boyfriend's set up an antiques business in Horsham.'

'Sounds expensive. Does Eva live in?'

'She only commutes at weekends and always stays with her mother. Seems Zita keeps her under her thumb. Maybe that's why the fiancé's setting up his new business only five miles down the road.'

'Whew! If he had any sense he'd steer well clear of the mother-in-law.'

'Perhaps Zita wouldn't let go. Tracey reckons she's a bad-tempered old biddy and there was that big row with Suzie in the post office which we've never got to the bottom of.'

Hayes rose and shuffled his papers into a briefcase. 'Well, keep at it, Prentice, we're not going to get much from DI Clarke it seems to me. I'll be back tonight – see you at seven, eh? Oh, and by the way, do you ride?'

Prentice stiffened. 'Er, well – yes, sir, I do.'

'Thought so. You look like a gal who'd shape up well on a hunter. Get Wickham to take you out for a canter on the downs. I can't believe an experienced man like him would disregard the careless saddling-up of a kid's pony. Keep it informal. By all accounts he fancies himself with the ladies, might loosen up his tongue having a nice blonde to show off to.'

Mo's eyes widened. This work was certainly different from her job with the Serious Fraud Office.

Thirteen

'Good morning. This is Detective Superintendent Hayes calling. Could I speak to Professor Klein? It's a personal call.'

He waited while the girl on the switchboard called through to Klein's office. 'Putting you through now, Superintendent.'

'Hi, Richard. Long time since, eh?'

'Precisely. I read about your run-in with the muggers in the summer. Back in the saddle already, Roger, or is this really a personal call? Some hope!'

Hayes laughed. 'You are such a suspicious sod, Richard. I'm ringing to see if you're free for lunch. I'm in the street below passing gold nuggets into the parking meter. Fancy our old haunt for a quick bite? I know you're always so busy but even boffins have to eat.'

'No strings?'

'Strictly old lags' reunion, believe me.'

'The Savoy Grill, you said?'

Hayes choked. 'I did *not*! But if you insist. If you put your skates on we can push in before the rush, OK?'

'Be right with you.'

Within ten minutes they were seated at a not too obvious corner table alternately eyeing each other and the menu with sharp curiosity.

'Wine?'

'Water for me, chum. I've got a seminar to chair this afternoon. Are you still working from Renham?'

'No. Promoted. I'm with the Met now, setting up a new unit. Very hush-hush.'

Klein's tanned features crinkled with amusement. '007 stuff?'

'More MI5,' Hayes countered with a grin. 'But seriously, Richard, it's been a long time. You still on that bacterio- logical-research project that hit the news last month?'

'Unfortunately yes. Not going smoothly but we're getting there. What are you going to have, Roger?'

'Scallops followed by a steak, I think. I need the energy.'

The waiter discreetly took their order, shuffling away silently as if on castors. The two men chatted for the next ten minutes before Hayes made his strike.

'This case I'm currently on. Strictly between ourselves, Richard, it's a bummer. You may have heard a little about it on the news but my boss is moving heaven and earth to keep the lid on it. The wife of an EU chap you probably know, Sir William Brigham, was murdered at their home in Sussex a few nights ago.'

'Mm, I seem to remember hearing something about it. I thought they were centred in Brussels.'

'He is, the wife not.'

'A violent intruder?'

'Can't say, but the local police are doing their best.'

'But you're with the Met now, you said.'

'Right. But I've been shunted down to the sticks to keep an eye on the investigation, to prevent any flak falling on Brigham's head.'

'He was at home when this happened?'

'No. It's a second marriage, something of a trophy wife, you know what I mean.'

Klein paused, sipping his sparkling water with an air of polite attention. 'So? Why are we expensively lunching together after all this time? I trust it is on expenses. And don't pull that one about the old pals' act, Roger, we are both too cynical to play silly buggers.'

'OK, to cut to the chase as they say, I'm far from sure what brings about these special security measures ring- fencing Brigham from any fallout. He was Chief Executive of Bluetex Pharmaceuticals before taking this EU job. Even in scientific circles that must have seemed a sideways move. You're in the loop research-wise, Richard. What's the story?'

'Off the record?'

'On my honour.'

Klein waited while the waiter served the main course, regarding the diners in the rapidly filling restaurant with the eye of a man more used to scanning germ particles under a microscope. He presented a powerful aura despite the gravy-spotted tie and tweeds, his domelike head polished like a nut, his penetrating gaze magnified behind thick lenses.

Roger attacked his fillet steak with gusto and bent his ear to catch his informant's low tones.

'Well, the research community is as gossip-ridden as an old ladies' whist drive, but more vicious. Bluetex Pharmaceuticals, Brigham's old outfit, was likely to make a mint with a new cancer cure called Rixolyn. Tests were running smoothly at first but a whiff of a smoke signal set knees knocking under the boardroom table in Berne, and Brigham was allegedly tipped off. He pulled some strings and scrambled out before the roof fell in. Only a few in government circles heard the reverberations and being a prominent party supporter Brigham copped a knighthood. Bluetex had to dump the entire project and compensate the poor suckers who were trialling the new drug.'

'People died?'

'One Chinese woman. It was cleverly hushed up. She was an illegal immigrant glad of the money. Brigham lost all credibility in the scientific world despite his nifty move to Europe. It was his only alternative.'

'But he's still under wraps? Still able to demand special protection from my security unit?'

Klein concentrated on picking the bones from his sole and remained silent.

'And that's *it*?' Roger persisted.

'Sufficient political influence to allow him a stone to crawl under.'

'Meaning me?' Hayes paused and the silence sifted around them like a chill breeze.

Klein looked up. 'Enough said, old man.'

'You're not suggesting Brigham's wife was killed in a

revenge attack, are you? A Chinese reprisal after the death of the unfortunate research victim? Triads?'

Klein burst out laughing, throwing himself back in his chair in hilarity. 'Good God, Roger, now you're really into the cloak-and-dagger stuff, aren't you? No, of course not. The poor Brigham woman was, like you said, killed by an intruder.'

'I didn't say that!'

'Well, it is the most obvious conclusion, isn't it? And now, let's have coffee. Can't offer you a cigarette I'm afraid but tell me all your news. Remarried? Still trying to play at being Liszt?'

Later, after he had dropped Richard Klein back at the university, Hayes rushed every yellow light to reach Elgin Mews in time for his appointment with the widower. If Sir William suffered any guilty feelings about his wife's death, digging around in the man's past would be difficult if not actually banned by Commander Crick. Political protection indeed? What next!

Elgin Mews was tucked away behind the square and parking without a residents' permit was impossible. In frustration Hayes, as a desperate measure, pulled a POLICE – ON EMERGENCY CALL card from under the dashboard and edged into the cobbled byway Brigham used as his London pied-à-terre.

Hayes was not surprised that Suzie preferred to stay home in Flodde with her horses. This tiny terraced establishment had little to recommend it save its own internal garage, the dirty white stucco flaky on this dismal October afternoon, the windows, closely shuttered, giving an abandoned air, the look of a little-used bolt-hole not so far removed from its original purpose, a convenient back-street shelter for one's motor car if not one's carriage.

The young man who opened the door held out a welcoming hand and introduced himself. 'Renton Brigham, sir. You must be the policeman I spoke to earlier. Do come in. A terrible business . . . poor old Suzie . . .'

Hayes waited for him to shut the door, the airlessness

of the living room coupled with its low ceiling seeming claustrophobic.

'I'm afraid my father had to go out, Superintendent. I tried to ring you but one of the constables said you had already left. Will I do?'

Fourteen

Hayes could barely contain his irritation. 'You do realize I have driven up from Flodde expressly to speak with Sir William?'

Young Brigham made a painful moue, his smooth cheeks puckering with sympathy. 'Yes, of course, Superintendent. Please accept his sincere apologies, he's a busy man.'

'And I'm not?' Hayes tartly retorted, then, deciding to make the best of it, smiled.

'Won't you come through, Superintendent? I've got the coffee on.'

Renton Brigham was good-looking, tall and muscular, a white T-shirt moulding his impressive pecs, navy jogging pants loosely defining what Hayes could only surmise to be marathon equipment.

He followed Renton into the kitchen, a narrow space no more than a galley where a percolator was indeed on the hob, mugs and sugar at the ready.

'Milk, Superintendent?'

'Black, no sugar. Thanks. I am told you are a fitness trainer, Mr Brigham.'

'Renny. Everyone calls me Renny. Yes, freelance. It leaves me plenty of spare time.'

'You have hobbies?'

'Photography. I'm taking a course. Hope to break into the fashion scene. Suzie introduced me to Fritz, her ex, and he's promised to take me on as an assistant if my portfolio stacks up.'

'Fritz Grice?'

'You've heard of him?'

Hayes grinned. 'I'm no Sussex plod, Renny.'

'No, of course you're not! Pa mentioned that the Met were sending down some auxiliary input to beef up the investigation. Shall we make ourselves comfortable? I'm sorry it's been a wasted journey for you but I expect you could do with a break.'

'Well, perhaps you can fill in some details for me now that I'm here. Do you live in the Mews?'

'Christ, no! I've got a pad in Prince of Wales Drive by the park.'

'Battersea.'

'That's right. My clients are mostly from the Chelsea area, so the park's convenient.'

'Many clients?'

'Eight at present. Too many really, especially as they mostly like to train before work.'

'Up at dawn, then.'

'Yes, that's the ticket. Some like to have a workout at home but I try to get them out for a run if I can. Clears the lungs.'

'Fascinating game. Mostly women, I suppose?'

'One bloke. A banker. But he has to be in the City before seven so now the mornings are darker we work out at the gym each day. He likes the discipline of having his own personal trainer, keeps him on the ball if you see what I mean.'

Hayes sipped his coffee and brought Brigham back to base. 'To help me with my enquiries, Renny, tell me about your stepmother. Popular, I gather.'

'Our Suzie? In the village, you mean? Well, she kept a low profile after her little pony-club venture folded but she had friends in London, of course, people she knew before she met my father.'

'Which was where?'

Renton shrugged. 'Not sure. At the races, I think – Ascot, probably. Suzie knew all about horses so they had a lot in common.'

'The riding accident didn't spoil her welcome in the village? The loss of the Kipling child?'

'Hell, no. It wasn't her fault. Riding's a dangerous game, never fancied it myself. I prefer skiing.'

'Your sister's keen, though. Has her own mount stabled at the Grange.'

'Eva's always been horse-mad, though not so much lately, not with the wedding in the offing.'

'When's that?'

'Well, it was scheduled for New Year's Eve but since Suzie's – er—'

'Murder.'

Renton flushed. 'Yeah, well, I expect Pa will want to delay things if he can persuade my mother to postpone her arrangements. People have already been invited, a heavy guest list including Pa's European contacts. It's going to be a bloody nightmare putting everything on hold.'

'You've spoken to Eva since your stepmother's death?'

'Not likely. Nothing I can say would be of any interest. Eva and Mother pull the strings in this family and if my father wants to cancel everything I wish him well. It's poor bloody Frederick I feel sorry for.'

'The fiancé?'

'Freddie MacCann, a mate of mine.' He brightened. 'I introduced them, in a manner of speaking.'

Hayes raised an eyebrow. 'How come?'

'Well, my sister, she's pretty square, not a party gal, so persuading her to go to one of my client's dating parties took some doing. There's nothing wrong with Eva,' he hastily added, 'just shy. And my mother tends to be something of a control freak. She wouldn't even let Eva have driving lessons, said the roads were too dangerous, which is rich considering my sister rides with the local hunt.'

'Your client who owns the dating agency, she employs you as her personal trainer?'

'Nothing heavy – just enough to keep her looking the part. Daphne runs this very exclusive dating racket called Match Point and sometimes I help out at the club cocktail dos if numbers are low. Every Monday at the Cuckoo Club in Mayfair. It's normally closed on Mondays so it was easy for Daphne to hire the place from five till seven.'

'*Cinq à sept*?' Hayes laughed. 'Like that French joke about fitting in adultery after work? Very ooh-la-la. So you sometimes go along to lighten up the age range? Most of the paying guests are older, I imagine; divorcees, rich widows, that sort of thing?'

'Daphne tries to even things out and when she suggested I introduce my sister to a bit of fun I wasn't too keen at first. But I was wrong. I dragged her along one night and she met Frederick so it must have been Fate, mustn't it?'

'Surely there's a hefty joining fee?'

'Absolutely. Daphne has a lot of expenses weeding out the weirdos.'

'But only a cocktail party? Doesn't give the punters much scope, does it?'

'You'd be surprised! Music, dancing, champagne: if they strike lucky it continues on to dinner for two or at least the theatre.'

'And you are a member?'

Renny laughed. 'Not me! As I said, I just fill in if Daphne thinks the clientele's a bit top heavy with the ladies. But Eva joined.'

'And Frederick was looking for a serious date?'

'Not at first. Daphne let him tag along for free a couple of times, he's a good-looking guy, and I more or less pushed my sister in his direction. Frederick's a smashing bloke but Match Point wouldn't normally be his scene. Too pricy.'

It sounded to Hayes as if Renny and his freebie mate were more like a couple of amateur gigolos, but what did he know about the current dating scene in Mayfair?

He reluctantly refocused: getting to Pimlico to update the Commander before driving back to Flodde would fit in nicely, and all in all, the journey hadn't altogether been wasted. He placed his mug on the coffee table and rose to go, holding out his hand to Renny.

'Well, thank you for the pit stop. Sorry to have missed Sir William but perhaps you would warn him that I shall require a meeting quite urgently. Have you any idea of his movements over the weekend?'

'Sorry, I'm just the messenger boy here, Superintendent.'

Hayes waited for Renny to open the front door but, pausing on the threshold, threw in an afterthought.

'Your mother, Lady Brigham, was nervous of allowing your sister to drive, you said. How did she get down to Sussex each weekend – by train?'

'Mum has a tab with a taxi firm, a regular booking to pick up Eva every Friday night from the station.'

'Good heavens, that sounds an impossible imposition on a young woman.'

'Like I said, my mother likes to be in charge and since she can no longer drive herself the regular pick-up has worked reasonably well for the past year.'

'She doesn't drive herself? Must make it difficult for her, living in the country.'

Renny looked sheepish. 'Well, you'll only find out for yourself from police records, so I might as well tell you. Mother got a drink-driving ban and is off the road at present.'

'She had an accident?'

'Oh no, just spotted swigging from a bottle of gin outside the post office in the village. Stupid, really, but she asked for it. We never found out who reported her, but, to be honest, it was a blessing in disguise. We all worried about her being half cut at the wheel.'

Hayes nodded and made a hasty retreat. No doubt about it, the Brighams were an interesting bunch.

Fifteen

He presented himself at the Pimlico headquarters with a stack of unanswered questions in his file. Unfortunately, the Commander was in conference and Bennet was out. He breezed in to Maurice Gibson's office to fill in until Crick was free.

His IT colleague was showing one of the trainees how he liked to file his personal case notes. Filing was, Hayes was all too aware, a picky subject but attention to detail would naturally be a 'must have' to any computer geek like Gibson. His own grasp of the technical know-how was hazy. Perhaps it was time he took an advanced course. Apart from the Brigham case the work for the new Melrose Unit was thin on the ground and setting up a date on the IT front would be very useful.

Gibson looked up, cheerfully banishing his acolyte to the filing department in the basement, leaving them alone. 'Well, how goes it, Roger? Solved the Brigham murder already?'

'I wish! Frankly, I'm not sure why we've been called in on this baby, the locals are perfectly capable of running their own show.'

'How's Mo Prentice shaping up?'

'Well.'

'She phoned me about Sir William. Asked me to snoop around.'

'Really? Funny thing is I called in to see a contact of mine today about the same thing. Professor Klein. You know him?'

'Not personally. Any fallout on Brigham?'

'Gossip in the research game indicates a thumbs-down

on his reputation over the Bluetex handling of the Rixolyn tests. A trial patient died.'

'Yes, I found some details about that myself. Faxed the info to Mo this morning. It seems Brigham shipped out just in time, left the rest of the board members to take the flak while he shimmied up the greasy pole in Brussels.'

'I'm totally green when it comes to commercial rivalry in the pharmaceutical line. Did you get the impression Bluetex was on to something with this new drug?'

Maurice Gibson was a circumspect sort, not given to rash judgement, and his sober response was suitably low key. 'They certainly cut a few corners but having competitors in that field makes for a race and jealousy may have coloured the condemnation of Brigham. Maybe he just got lucky, getting out by the skin of his teeth like he did.'

'Perhaps his support within the party had something to do with it. He must be a smooth operator to command political backing at top level, which is presumably why Crick got us involved. You never came across Brigham in your previous job with the Ministry, Maurice?'

Gibson shook his head. 'Saw him once at a do to celebrate our lucky winner of the Nobel Prize for Chemistry a little while ago and, frankly, I was impressed. He should have been a diplomat. And has an easy style with the ladies, too, a tasty young woman on his arm who I presume was the wife who died.'

'Mm. Now, don't shoot me down in flames, Maurice, but would you say Brigham moved in the sort of waters where a hit man would swim?'

Gibson recoiled. 'Paid a professional to kill his wife, you mean? Why would he do that?'

'Well, it seems the second Lady Brigham was a bit of a goer on the quiet. Probably not the sort of girl to leave to twiddle her thumbs at home in the country while he was in Europe for most of the year. Also, a young wife like Suzie Brigham could be expensive. Liked horses for a start, always a ritzy hobby, and alimony for the ex must stack up. I've just been to his London home and it's not the sort of place I would expect a bloke like Brigham to have. Did your trawl through the background stuff for Prentice come up with anything?'

'Nothing concrete. His first wife was an operatic star in her heyday, you know. Zita de Lazlo. Born in Hungary but brought up in London. Sang with all the top companies but marrying Brigham seemed to put the lid on her career.'

'She's taken to gin in her autumn years.'

Gibson frowned. 'Good God, Roger, you've really dredged the pool on this case, haven't you? No real evidence, though. No leads?'

The door opened and a young constable put his head round. 'The Commander's free now, Superintendent.'

Hayes nodded. 'Be right there.' He turned back to Gibson. 'One more thing, Maurice. Could you run a check on a dating agency called Match Point? A woman called Daphne something or other owns it and operates a cocktail party for loners every Monday evening at the Cuckoo Club. See what you can fish up, would you, please?'

'I'll get on to it straight away. Call in on your way out after you've reported in with the Commander and I'll have some printouts ready for you. Presumably there's a website?'

'Can't say. It's pretty exclusive, by all accounts. I'm not sure how these agencies advertise themselves.'

'Leave it with me, Rog.'

It was almost seven before Hayes got back to the Red Lion. He found Mo Prentice in the bar with a tumbler of some sort of fizzy concoction tarted up with sprigs of mint and slices of lemon. She looked pretty full of herself, her eyes lighting up at his appearance.

'Had a good day, Prentice?'

'Not bad. And you, sir?'

'Bloody frustrating. Brigham wasn't there, the Commander was in conference and the traffic driving back was practically bumper to bumper. Can't understand how these people commute from here each day, it must be hell. Did you fix up anything with the Brighams over the weekend?'

'Tea at Lady Brigham's on Sunday.'

Hayes grimaced.

'With Eva and possibly her fiancé. And I found out about that row Zita had with our victim in the village post office.'

'Don't drive me too far, Prentice. I'm up to my eyes in local gossip as it is.'

'Actually this is interesting, sir. Suzie was verbally attacked about Eva's horse. She had arranged for Denzil – that's the horse, sir – to be shipped out to the stud farm in Ireland. No warning to Eva, and Wickham admitted to me that she had already decided a month ago to send *all* the horses back to the stud farm in due course.'

'And what happens to Wickham, our so-called stable manager? Has he got notice to quit?'

'Far from it. He's going back to Ireland too. Sir William's promised him promotion, more money and a nice new house to boot. Strikes me Sir William decided to sell up here weeks ago and relocate permanently to Brussels. But Wickham said it was all to be kept hush-hush until after the wedding, not even Tracey is in on these plans.'

Hayes let out a deep breath. 'Excellent work, Prentice. How did you winkle all this out of Wickham? Poor old DI Clarke knows nothing about it, or else he's been keeping me in the dark.'

'No, Wickham says he was told to keep it quiet. To say, if anyone asked, that Denzil, Eva's horse, was just going to the stud farm temporarily and to let slip nothing to anyone about a possible sale of the Grange. We took out two of the horses like you suggested, sir. Worked a treat, couldn't stop himself bragging about the big money he's going to earn once he moves back to Ireland.'

Sixteen

'Let's move into the snug, Prentice. It's quieter and I could do with a drink before we go in for dinner. You OK with that horrible fizzy stuff?' he said, indicating Mo's teetotal cocktail.

He joined her in a side room where a log fire burned brightly in the hearth. They settled at one of the small tables each set with a bar menu and wooden place mats printed with hunting scenes. Hayes had to admit he'd lodged at worse billets on police duty but working cheek by jowl with a female detective made him uncomfortable. He had been used to a macho team backing up any investigation but the Melrose Unit was something else. Not that he had any complaints about Sergeant Prentice who, it must be said, fitted into the Brigham milieu like a dream, what with her crystal vowels and ability to put her very attractive arse up on a big stallion like Denzil.

'OK. Tell me more about this rumour that Brigham had planned to sell up even before his wife's death.'

'More than a rumour, sir, I'd swear Wickham was on the level and I checked with the blacksmith at the forge in the village. Got chatting about his business prospects since the hunting ban came into force and he was perfectly sanguine about it. Said the local hunt would get round it somehow. I casually asked about Denzil, mentioned I'd been given a ride on an exercise gallop with Wickham and waxed all enthusiastic about the Brigham stables. The smith, a bloke called Ben Thornton, reckoned Denzil was a dangerous beast, too frisky for eventing and as much as even Eva could handle. "Better off in Ireland at the stud farm," he said, though quickly assuring me it was only a temporary measure.

He'd been booked to reshoe Denzil but Wickham had cancelled, admitting that the horse was being transported this coming week though Thornton wondered whether the transfer would be delayed since Lady Brigham's death.'

'He thought it was all Suzie's idea?'

'Yes. Apparently she didn't trust Denzil, but Thornton reckoned the friskiness had more to do with the way Wickham handled the horse and the fact that it was not getting enough hard exercise since Eva stopped going to the stables every weekend.'

'But it *is* Eva's horse?'

'Her father actually owns it, Wickham says. Has every right to sell it if he wants to though Thornton didn't say anything about the other horses going to Ireland as well. I think Wickham was indiscreet telling me that, it would have been a big drop in income if Thornton lost Sir William's horses, he'd been disappointed enough when Suzie's ponies were sold off after the Kipling child's death.'

'In the course of this heart-to-heart at the forge, did Thornton offer any opinion about the accident?'

Mo shook her head. 'I tried to draw him out but he wouldn't bite. "All old history, miss," he said, "best forgot."'

'So how did Zita get to hear about Eva's horse being shipped out? I thought it was all hush-hush?'

'Difficult to keep secrets in a place like this, and if Wickham can be gabby with a stranger like me, he might have bragged about it in the pub. Thornton wasn't giving anything away. The Brighams are influential with the hunt crowd, he wouldn't want to get into their bad books.'

'OK. Keep at it, girl, you've obviously got a knack with these guys. Any joy from Tracey?'

Mo slurped the dregs from her glass and attacked a bag of crisps, frowning with concentration.

'Not so lucky there, sir. I probably approached it from the wrong angle, questioning her assurance about Suzie's popularity in the village.'

'Wickham inviting you out for a canter wouldn't endear her, I bet.'

'You think so?' Mo seemed surprised and Hayes wondered

if this girl appreciated what a threat she might present to a simple kid like Tracey Wilson. 'Well, sir, I said I'd heard about the Kipling tragedy and that Mrs Cosham seemed not too heartbroken about Suzie's death. "She's an old bitch. Never took to Suzie from the start, bullied her rotten, always insisting everything had to be done as Zita had it."'

'Her exact words?'

'Near enough. I asked about Denzil going to Ireland but she clammed up so I switched to her work at the big house. Like Mrs Cosham said, Tracey's duties were hardly onerous. She vacuumed round, did a bit of dusting and kept the bedrooms ready for unexpected guests.'

'Any comment about the sleeping arrangements?'

'Suzie and Sir William, you mean? I asked her about that and she said the old boy sometimes slept in his dressing room if he came home late from the airport, but there was no suggestion of any rift.'

'No overheard rows?'

'She doesn't live in, sir. Tracey wouldn't be about when they were alone. Suzie didn't run to a maid or a butler, you'd have to ask the housekeeper. It was all very informal unless extra staff were drafted in for weekend parties.'

'But Mrs Kipling had a regular job doing the laundry? Was there any suspicion that Suzie's bed had entertained a stranger during Brigham's absence? Backstairs chitchat?'

'I skirted round it, making out it was just my nasty curiosity, but if Mrs Kipling got any idea of that sort she wasn't sharing it with a kid like Tracey, who was pretty starstruck by their new mistress and wouldn't say a word against her.'

'Perhaps you should tackle Mrs Kipling directly.'

'Might work. It's a pity the proposed sale of the big house isn't out in the open, sir. If the squire was known to be upping sticks, the locals wouldn't be so wary about causing trouble. As it is they keep their opinions between themselves. Wickham's an outsider but the rest of 'em's as thick as thieves.'

'But I can't see how Mrs Kipling could continue to carry on working there after her daughter had died in the grounds.

Surely the place would haunt her? The poor woman showed no animosity towards her employer?'

'If there was any tension, Suzie was wise enough to ignore it. Tracey reckons Cosham and the Kipling woman are hand-in-glove, born and bred in the village like herself and presenting a bold front in the face of an incomer like Suzie. Perhaps they were hoping she wouldn't last long.'

'Well, if they put any money on it they were damn right. Seems to me poor bloody Suzie walked into a snake pit taking Zita's place in a house she'd called home for most of her married life. Did you get the impression from Wickham that it was Suzie's idea to sell up?'

'He reckoned not. He said it was Sir William's plan, though she was the one who wanted the horses moved to Ireland straight away.'

'With your know-how in the Serious Fraud Office, could you suss out any financial shenanigans in Brigham's career? Any shares dispute with Bluetex? Any cash settlement to cover his sudden departure? Dodgy insider trading prior to the crash following the death of the Chinese trial patient?'

She looked pensive. 'I could ask around.'

'Oh, and by the way, I called in to see Maurice while I was at headquarters. He said you'd been on to him for more background stuff on Brigham.' Hayes bent down to extract papers from his document case. 'Here, browse through this lot, Prentice. If we are going to tea with the Zita faction on Sunday the stuff about the dating agency where Eva met her fiancé's interesting. I'll tell you about my chat with Renton Brigham over dinner. I'm starving, let's go and eat.'

Seventeen

To give DI Clarke his due, Hayes could not fault him on overtime. Sunday morning found him still hard at it in the incident room, and a full team drafted in to cover door-to-door enquiries to chase up any sightings of strangers or even suspicious residents hanging about on Wednesday night.

'You've searched the grounds again, I see,' Hayes remarked. 'Any luck, Inspector?'

'Apart from the paint fragments dug out from the tree and the tyre marks which may line up with a red sports car? Hardly a vehicle to go unnoticed round here. The difficulty is that the Grange is set well away from the village and can be approached from several side roads. Incidentally, we ran a check on the semen sample found on the body. It doesn't link with any DNA on the criminal database.'

Hayes slumped in a chair on the other side of the partners' desk. 'I had a wasted journey myself yesterday. Arranged to see Sir William at his home but he'd skipped. It's five days since the murder, Clarke, and I haven't managed to pin him down so far. You been luckier?'

Clarke shuffled the files on his desk, avoiding Hayes' scrutiny. 'Not really. Superintendent Fox and I cornered him on Thursday at the mortuary but it hardly seemed the right moment to question a widower about his movements.'

Hayes' mouth hardened. 'Well, I shall have to get backing from my own boss and insist on an interview. You have met him before, I expect. On less melancholy occasions?'

'Only once. My boy was keen to join Lady Brigham's pony club but Sir William refused, quite brusquely now you mention it, insisted that all the places were taken.'

'Mostly by little girls, I imagine.'

'Yes, but I got the feeling he wasn't impressed with the kids larking about in his paddock at all which, as it turned out, showed some forebodings.'

'Do you think he was worried about the way Wickham and Lady B. were handling it?'

'He trusted Wickham, no question about that, but he's been overly protective of his new wife, wanting to spare her any criticism from his daughter Eva, who fancied herself as a much better horsewoman and made no secret of it.'

'No love lost there, then. But Brigham jumped through hoops to get Suzie accepted within the family, didn't he? Spared no expense. Hosted a big party for Eva's engagement, stabled her horse and so on.'

'Well, who can blame him? No father wants to lose the affection of his children. Perhaps he felt this new baby on the horizon would bind the family together.'

Hayes rather doubted this, but persisted. 'You may be right but I can only say that Sir William's evasions look bad. I shall have to insist on his cooperation.'

'He might want a lawyer present.'

'His solicitor? Why? I'm not accusing the man, not yet anyway. But the more he keeps his head down, the greater my concern. Anyone would think I wasn't on his side! I've only been dragged in on this case to see fair play. But my sergeant and I have at least acquired a meeting with Lady Zita, and hopefully Eva too, this afternoon. I shall be interested to see if the prospective son-in-law is wheeled out. A Mr Frederick MacCann. Have you met him?'

'Not yet, but I've seen his van buzzing round. Black with gold lettering. Very smart.'

'Has a business in the town, I gather.'

'Antiques. Accommodation over the shop and situated right in the centre too. Should do well. Not my line exactly but the missus has been in for a snoop round. Expensive tat.'

'Even so, it must have cost a bit to set up in the Square. Rent alone, apart from the stock. Maybe Sir William's helping out to get the chap started.'

'Part of the reconciliation package? You may be right, sir. The son and heir wasted no time buttering up his new stepmother.'

'I met Renton at the London pad. Seems nice enough and certainly got on well with Suzie Brigham – she had already introduced him to her contacts in the modelling game. He plans to be a fashion photographer.'

A constable hovered at the door, waiting patiently to put in a word. Hayes left Clarke to it and alerted Prentice on his mobile to be ready for a final look round the Grange. 'Mrs Cosham's been given the all-clear. She's moving back into the house tomorrow with her team of domestics. Making it shipshape for the master's return.'

'Brigham's moving back? Who told you that?'

'Tracey. I caught her mucking out the stables this morning. She was pretty miffed at not being included in the spring clean.'

'Clarke said nothing about Sir William coming down here and he knew I was busting a gut to get an interview, blast him.'

Mo buttoned her lip, all too aware that putting her spoke in would only make matters worse.

'Well, move yourself, girl, let's go over the crime scene before the housekeeper and her gang clear whatever evidence may still remain. Oh, and while you're on, what did the coroner's officer say about the Kipling inquest?'

'He doesn't work weekends, sir. But I'll get on to it first thing in the morning.' She held the phone away from her ear as Hayes let rip before cutting the connection on a final blast of frustration.

Apart from a constable on the front door and the gardener working in the back, Aspern Grange was deserted. Hayes impatiently waited for Mo Prentice, pacing the house front like a lean and hungry wolf searching for a way in.

She arrived late, pedalling up the drive, her hair bunched up under a hard hat, and swerved to an untidy halt. She leaned the cycle against the wall and greeted the constable with a wry grin.

'Christ Almighty, Prentice, what have you got there? The district nurse's pushbike?'

'It's all right for you, sir, you've got the car. Getting round on foot was a waste of time. Hedgecoe arranged for me to borrow a bike from the station on the condition I wore this awful headgear. Any chance of renting a spare vehicle next week, sir? If I'm to get into town to see the coroner's officer on Monday I don't want to hire a taxi and you'll need the car yourself.'

She balanced the crash helmet on the saddle and uncoiled a long striped scarf knotted at her throat. Her cheeks were flushed to a rosy glow which might not, Hayes considered, be merely the result of a brisk pull uphill from the village, but irritation only barely held in check.

'You're right, one vehicle's not enough. I thought we'd be out of here by now but the difficulty of lining up all these bloody people is dragging everything out. Anyway, let's go inside and turn the place over privately without Hedgecoe on our heels. Take it slowly, Prentice, and look at everything with a fresh eye as if we had never seen the crime scene before. Got it? You take the stairs and hallway and I'll check the first floor.'

Hayes took the stairs two at a time and surveyed the victim's bedroom anew. A shaft of sunlight pierced a gap in the half-drawn curtains with the clarity of a laser beam, focusing on the stripped bed with indecent attention. Hayes worked the room methodically, shining his torch under the bed, easing the side cabinets from the wall, upending drawers and meticulously searching all the pockets of Suzie's jackets and jeans hanging in the bank of wardrobes. Nothing. Not even a discarded receipt in any of her numerous designer handbags. He then checked Sir William's adjoining dressing room with equal lack of success.

The bathroom proved more instructive, however. Clarke's men had obviously trawled through the contents of the medicine cabinet which were, interestingly, almost exclusively Sir William's, including, Hayes was amused to note, a bottle of men's hair dye. But no pharmaceutical products from Bluetex. Perhaps Brigham had fallen out of love with his former employer or maybe knew too much about placebos to be impressed by the ads.

Suzie's stuff comprised mostly bath essences and jars of night cream and cleansers, her make-up concentrated in the dressing-table drawers in the bedroom. Apart from a modest supply of aspirins and a small bottle of herbal sleeping pills, the only surprising item on Suzie's shelf was a half-used strip of oral contraceptives hidden in a box of tissues.

So . . . If Sir William had been pining for a new heir to the questionable Brigham fortune, his beautiful young wife had other ideas. But Silly Suzie had been careless. Got herself pregnant all the same . . .

Eighteen

Lady Brigham's residence dominated the main street and was indeed impressive, the entrance opening directly onto the pavement, blue shutters flanking the sashed windows: a most generous new home for an ex.

'Crikey,' Mo exclaimed. 'This place must have cost a bomb.'

'Divorces come expensive,' Hayes muttered with feeling as he rang the bell.

The door was opened almost immediately by a slim dark girl in jeans and a beige sweater who examined their warrant cards with no apparent emotion at all, before ushering them through to the drawing room.

Zita occupied a gold brocade sofa, her jet-black hair fashioned into a lacquered helmet, and looking vaguely like Imelda Marcos. Mo hovered in the background while Hayes stiffly introduced himself, the cool appraisal of the Brigham women giving the impression of an audience with royalty.

Suddenly the ice was broken by the invasion of a pair of noisy pugs which circled Zita's sofa like wind-up toys.

'Oh, Eva, I thought you'd locked them in the scullery!'

'Elsie must have let them out. They're all right, Mother, let them stay. Shall I ask Elsie to make the tea?'

Zita nodded, setting her drop earrings a-jiggle. She was a large woman, all dolled up in a red silk dress and patent shoes of which narrow straps cut sharply into her plump ankles. 'Do sit down, Superintendent – and your young assistant too, of course. Though how I can possibly help with your enquiries defeats me,' she said, indicating the matching sofa with a queenly gesture, her words subtly accented. A former opera star, Hayes remembered, and still living the part.

The dogs subsided onto a bean bag by the fire, their bug-eyed gaze watchful. The tall girl left the room, returning after a few minutes pushing a trolley laden with cakes and tea cups. She continued to remain wordless, pouring the tea and then passing a cup first to her mother and then to their unwelcome guests.

'You must be Miss Brigham,' Mo blurted out at last, unwilling to sit out this silent treatment.

'My daughter Eva,' Zita agreed. 'We spend every weekend here together. Eva prefers living in the country.'

'But you work in London, I believe,' Hayes put in, watching the girl with interest.

'Yes.' And that was it. Mo decided that interviewing this monosyllabic madam was going to be uphill work. She put aside her teacup and produced a notebook, waiting for Hayes to shake things up.

'As this is an official interview, I must ask you to be specific, Miss Brigham. Your address and place of employment, please.'

Zita attempted to intervene but Eva cut her off with a dismissive sweep of the hand. 'No problem, Superintendent, the sooner we dispose of your questions the better. I am sure you have more important things to do than sit here drinking tea.' She rattled off her personal details, her manner businesslike. 'And how else may I assist you?'

'Lady Brigham here mentioned that you regularly come down here at weekends. And sometimes stay with your fiancé?'

Zita stiffened but Eva swiftly listed her usual routine. 'No, I prefer to stay with Mother. I leave work on Friday evenings about eight and take the train which gets me home in time for supper. Frederick generally joins us after closing the shop on Saturday afternoon and on Sundays we sometimes go for a drive together before lunch.'

'Your fiancé doesn't ride?'

'Frederick!' She laughed, her face lighting up, the girl who Hayes had initially thought plain and unattractive suddenly blooming like a Japanese paper flower expanding in a glass of water. Not such a dog after all.

'No, Superintendent, my fiancé is allergic to horses, they get him sneezing in moments. Sad, but frankly I've rather lost my passion for riding lately.'

'Oh, I love it,' Mo exclaimed. 'Actually, I was given a ride on Denzil this week. Mr Wickham offered to take me for a gallop on the downs.' Her voice petered out under Hayes' stern look and all eyes focused on Eva, who had suddenly paled, her warm expression frozen.

'Wickham let you ride Denzil?' she spluttered. 'But he's *my* horse! What right did he—?' she gasped, then, speechless, bolted from the room.

'You must excuse my poor girl,' Zita smoothly put in, 'she's rather emotional at present – the wedding, you know.'

'Is it postponed?'

'I have yet to discuss arrangements with Sir William. I can't myself see why it can't go ahead, invitations have already been accepted, the wedding list is posted with Asprey's.'

'Sir William returns here soon, I understand.'

'Does he?' She frowned. 'Nobody tells me anything these days but I suppose this ghastly calamity at the Grange puts a new complexion on everything.'

'What does Mr MacCann think?'

'Frederick? I've no idea. Eva hasn't seen him yet – the new shop, you know, it takes up all his time at present. He's coming to dine this evening, we shall have to make a decision very soon. Perhaps,' she said, brightening, 'Sir William will join us? I shall ring him and see.'

Mo drew back, far from certain how much of all this was relevant to the investigation, but Hayes appeared to be unperturbed by the odd reaction to Suzie's murder, which seemed to be merely regarded as an inconvenience.

Hayes coughed. 'As you were saying, Lady Brigham, your daughter is upset by the turn events have taken, not helped, I expect, by the news that her horse is being sent to Ireland.'

'Absolutely! William never even mentioned it – I only heard about it from Mrs Cosham, my former housekeeper you know. All Suzie's doing, of course. She might have had the grace to ask Eva's permission before arranging it.'

'But Denzil *is* Sir William's property, isn't it?' Hayes gently persisted.

'Technically, I suppose, but it has always been Eva's horse. I am really surprised that Wickham allowed your sergeant to ride Denzil – it's a fiery mount.'

'Needs plenty of exercise, I bet, more than Wickham can cope with alone. The two other horses? Your son's?'

'William keeps a filly for hacking but Renton seldom rides.'

'And Miss Brigham mentioned a lack of enthusiasm for it since her engagement.'

'Well, yes and no. You know how these young girls are once love is in the air. Frederick blew her right off her feet, her first real romance, and all Renton's doing really.'

'Really?'

'Introduced them at a party in London. Persuaded Eva to go along with him. Between you and me, Superintendent,' she confided, 'my daughter's not much of a social butterfly, and the proposal came out of the blue.'

'But you approved of Mr MacCann?'

Zita dabbed her lips with the napkin. 'Well, not at first, but William persuaded me it would be a good match. I shall be very lonely without her,' she admitted, her eyes bright with unshed tears. She roused herself and glanced at the sleeping pooches. 'But I have my darling doggies and Eva will be living over the shop after the wedding, not far away from her mama after all.'

'And Renton? You see your son each weekend too?'

'Not every weekend. But since I no longer drive Renny comes by when I need him. To go to the theatre or shopping in Brighton and so on.'

'Eva doesn't drive?'

'Eva prefers her bicycle, says a car is an encumbrance in town. We have an account with the taxi people at the station though lately she has been bringing her bicycle with her, enjoys the ride home you see. But now the nights are drawing in I expect she will go back to using a taxi, that is if Frederick doesn't whisk her away from under my nose.'

'One more thing, Lady Brigham. You employed Mrs

Cosham for several years, I understand. What was your
opinion of her?'

Zita looked startled by the question, her heavily mascara'd
eyes widening in alarm. 'She's in no trouble, is she? Not
a suspect in this awful attack? I know she was bitter about
losing her staff cottage, but . . .'

'A routine enquiry, I assure you. You found Mrs Cosham
easy to get along with?'

She hurriedly rose from her seat and made clumsy steps
towards a console table where bottles and tumblers were
set out on a tray. 'I like a little cocktail at this time, don't
you? A low point in the day, I always think. Won't you
join me, Mr Hayes?'

'Not just now, thank you.'

She poured a stiff gin and tonic, ignoring the ice bucket,
and took a gulp before returning to the sofa.

'Cosham originally came to me as a children's nurse,
you know. Worked as a nanny before starting at the Grange,
but I think she found babies rather exhausting, looking after
my children was easier. She only took on the housekeeping
duties when they went away to school.'

'She was good with children? I only ask because I have
found her manner rather terse.'

'Oh, no, not at all. She loves kiddies. Took a shine to
young Rosie Kipling and persuaded Suzie to allow her to
join her little pony club. Rosie came from a rather poor
family, you see, Kipling was our mole-catcher and
handyman so having a chance to ride was a dream come
true for little Rosie. A tragic accident. I believe Cosham
blamed herself, thought it was her fault pushing the child
forward like she did. Broke her heart. Never had children
of her own, you see, and her husband died young leaving
her to make her own living as best she could.'

Zita grew thoughtful, sipping her gin with a faraway
look which Hayes impatiently broke into with a muttered
word of sympathy. He finished his tea, now tepid, and rose
to go.

'Well, we mustn't outstay our welcome, Lady Brigham.
You have been very kind. We shall not need to speak with

your daughter again but before I go perhaps you could confirm when she got back here on Friday.'

'Oh, the usual time. Just after nine. Elsie, our cook, leaves a casserole in the oven on Fridays in case the trains are delayed. The service is not what it was.' She turned to Mo, extending her hand like an empress. 'So nice to meet you, my dear. You are not at all my idea of a detective, if I may say so, but then I have to rely on the television so much these days and the women on these police shows are not at all ladylike, are they?'

They moved to the hall, Zita leading like a ship in full sail, clearly glad of an audience of any sort, even two questioning police officers.

Hayes paused on the threshold, chancing one last attack on the bulwarks of this strange family. 'Sir William must be utterly devastated at the loss of his wife and unborn child in such tragic circumstances.'

Zita's hand flew to her cheek. 'Unborn child? You are mistaken, Superintendent. My husband will father no more children. He underwent a vasectomy twenty years ago.'

Nineteen

Hayes took over the wheel and drove straight to Horsham, parking in a side street a hundred yards from the market square. The dull afternoon had slipped into early evening gloom, a persistent drizzle driving the few pedestrians to huddle in a bus shelter, the streetlights reflected in the puddles like an oil slick.

'Well, what did you make of that, Prentice?'

'Do you think it's true, sir? That bit about Sir William's vasectomy? Puts Suzie's pregnancy under a cloud.'

'He could have had the operation reversed, of course. It's not unknown to work, and if he was keen to top up the family tree or placate his wife's requirements on the baby front there could be some IVF input.'

Mo was sceptical. 'Will you ask him about it?'

'Got to catch the blighter first. But if Suzie invited a cuckoo in the nest, I can't see Brigham taking a kindly view, can you? The Commander promised to insist on an interview so Brigham can't dodge the investigation much longer.'

'But he has an alibi.'

'Yes, sure. Checked out of Brussels on Thursday morning after a full day's conference in Strasbourg which accounts for the previous twenty-four hours. Even so, we were only brought in to "protect the man from press intrusion", whatever that means, so it's only right that he gives us a statement. Now, let's mooch about and get some idea of this town. I want to dig out Frederick MacCann if I can. Look, there's his shop. Excellent site: it should do well.'

They peered in the window, the display of antique pieces attractively spotlit, the interior draped from view. Hayes

Vivien Armstrong

rang the bell and Mo stationed herself at the kerb watching the open curtains of the upstairs flat. They waited and he rang again, a persistent peal this time.

'No lights on, sir. Must be out.'

'On his way to Lady Brigham's, perhaps. Poor bloody MacCann will have his work cut out if he wants to delay the wedding. Let's take a dekko round the back.'

They slipped into an alleyway dividing the row of shops and found themselves in a narrow lane where cars stood bumper to bumper. MacCann's new van with its gleaming gold lettering was parked close to the brick wall which bordered the gardens behind the shop premises. Hayes shone his torch inside, mildly surprised by the neatness of the van's interior, and made a note of the registration number.

'New,' Mo remarked, running a finger along the lettering.

'Either our lad's keeping his head down or he's gone to the pub. The Brigham women don't drive, so unless he got a lift there, he's gone AWOL.'

'Got the train to London? Didn't Lady B. say MacCann was chummy with the brother?'

'Renton? Yeah, and Sunday would be his first chance to get away from the shop to share his troubles with a mate. Perhaps there's a conference with his prospective father-in-law to thrash out the wedding postponement.'

'Without the women?'

'Absolutely. Can you imagine getting anywhere with Zita and Eva screaming their heads off? Let's push off, we're going nowhere getting soaked standing here. There's a pizza place I noticed on the way in – let's take a break.'

They settled at a corner table, the place already noisy with kids. 'Escaping the rain,' Mo remarked with sympathy. Hayes was unperturbed by the racket, confident that here at least they could never be overheard. They ordered and Mo settled back with her glass of mineral water and waited for the boss's blue mood to clear. The difficulty of steering his own enquiries between the unseen obstacles the local police seemed to be placing in his path was getting to him, and Mo had quickly learned to be patient.

Hayes took a generous swig of lager and attacked the fragrant mozzarella ensemble with enthusiasm.

'Did you get anywhere with that Bluetex share-dealing idea? No rumours in your financial-shark waters about any government official benefiting from a tip-off from Brigham?'

'I put out a few feelers, sir, but the press correspondents are the ones more likely to spill any scandal and I dare not alert my private contacts in the money market when our brief is to protect Brigham from the media, not to stir the pot ourselves.'

'Mm, right. It's a bloody minefield out there, Prentice, and tiptoeing round the reason Brigham abandoned Bluetex so precipitously could bring the roof down on our heads. No wonder that slimy sod Bennet wanted to shift this investigation onto me, it has all the makings of an unexploded bomb.'

'To be fair, sir, taking up a senior post with the EU doesn't necessarily spell a drop in gross income, the perks can be substantial.'

Hayes frowned. 'Go on.'

'Well, sir, there's flash accommodation on offer if you're well up the ladder, which would explain why Sir William only keeps a modest pied-à-terre in London, not to mention ambassadorial residences costing millions of pounds in rents alone. The total budget is mind-blowing.'

'But he's not an EU ambassador.'

'Even so, changing jobs does not automatically signal a fall from grace, and for all we know Brigham's on a short list for promotion.'

Hayes looked sceptical but had to admit that pushing Prentice onto his team was probably a clever move by bloody Bennet, and if the girl knew her stuff and had useful contacts from her stint with the Serious Fraud Office, who was he to complain?

'OK. I get the message, but let's get back to basics. Brigham is fireproof and it's his wife's murder we're investigating, so let's scratch the surface locally, shall we? Did Hedgecoe come up with any details about phone calls to and from Suzie the night she died?'

'Not so far, sir, but no one's been hauled in on suspicion so my guess is they've drawn a blank. How about Wickham?'

'He's refused to offer a DNA sample.'

'Gosh! Surely that only puts him in the frame?'

'Without supporting evidence it's impossible for Clarke to insist. He has eliminated Lennie Kipling as Suzie's lover, which was never on the cards in the first place, but that doesn't mean Kipling didn't push his way into the house later and bash her on the head, does it? Clarke's still checking up on his movements but I can't see Kipling as a serious suspect two years after his kid died.'

'Minds fester, sir, and not being able to find another job wouldn't help. Also, if his wife's employed at the Grange she'd be anxious to keep the lid on any violent threats against Suzie he may have made.'

Hayes sighed. 'I need to talk to her doctor. Can you get hold of her address book? I presume Clarke claimed it together with her personal stuff. No hope of a diary, I suppose? Bloody hell, Prentice, how am I supposed to work this case with one hand tied behind my back?' He irritably summoned the waiter and called for the bill.

As Mo collected her wet mac from the row of hooks behind the cashier's desk, Hayes' phone shrilled. But by the time they were seated in the car his mood had lifted.

'I've got a date with Brigham – eleven o'clock in the morning. At his solicitor's office in Lincoln's Inn. Well, waddya know? I do believe we've rattled his cage, Prentice.'

Twenty

'What's the plan for tomorrow, sir? I've got an appointment with the coroner's officer first thing.'

'OK, I get the message: you want the car. No sweat. I'd prefer to take the train anyhow, I've a little excursion in mind for Monday night.'

'Me too?'

Hayes glanced at her profile, the jaw set in an attitude he had learned to read: Prentice in a stubborn mood.

He grinned. 'Come to think of it, that's not such a bad idea. How do you fancy a bit of undercover police work?'

She briefly took her eye off the road and shrugged. 'What sort of "undercover"?'

'I had intended to drop in on this dating agency myself, but on second thoughts you'd probably get more joy from it than I would. How does it strike you?'

'Can't say I've any experience, sir. What would I have to do?'

Hayes outlined the game played weekly at the Cuckoo Club in Mayfair. 'From five till seven, nothing heavy, just a drinks party where hopefuls can meet fellow members. It's called Match Point and is run by a woman Renton Brigham knows through his day job.'

'Which is?'

'Personal trainer. I gather that this woman occasionally netted Renton and his friend Frederick MacCann to make up numbers, provide a bit of muscle to tweak up the male intake.'

'I wouldn't have to dress up in a bunny outfit and act "hostess", would I?'

'Of course not! It's an expensive club. Renton persuaded his sister to join.'

'She was looking for romance?'

'Hit the bullseye right off. It was there she met her fiancé.'

'And you want me to mingle? Swan around and see what I can pick up?'

He laughed. 'Well, not literally. The point is the lads won't recognize you if they happen to be there tomorrow night whereas Renton for one would spot me a mile off. Chances are you'll learn nothing but I'm curious about the set-up. And a nice-looking girl like you could be a perfect honey trap. Are you on?'

'Fine. But what's the downside, sir?'

'Plain sailing, I promise you. You don't have to worry about going on with anyone afterwards, if that's what's bothering you. Shall I fix it with this Daphne person? I'm sure she'll cooperate if I say it's just a general sweep to mop up any dirty dicks we have on our books, might even be grateful.'

Mo looked askance. 'You're not thinking Suzie was a member, are you?'

'It's a possibility. She was very close to Renton and we've run out of any likely boyfriends in the local area. I can try to get a word with her ex, the photographer, Fritz Grice, while I'm in town. He might have an idea about Suzie's old dates from her modelling days. She was left alone at home far too much for a trophy wife looking as stunning as she did. What a waste! I don't buy all this guff about the new lady of the manor being totally satisfied with country life and the Sussex horsey set. Here, drop me off at the incident room, Prentice. I need to shake down Clarke for the doctor's address. Do you want to think over this little expedition on the dating front?'

'No way. Sounds fun. Shall I drive up after I've seen the coroner's man and meet you about four o'clock? I can stop off at home on the way and see you afterwards to drive back here. That's if you intend to come back tomorrow night, sir.'

'Let's play it by ear. You do the local enquiries and I'll meet you at headquarters in the afternoon and put you in the picture after I've spoken to the Match Point lady.' He paused. 'Perhaps it would be a good idea to keep our little plan under wraps from Bennet for the time being. He may have other ideas.'

'How do I explain my glad rags?'

'Blimey, Prentice, use your initiative! Say you've got a date if anyone asks, which is unlikely, they're not exactly observant these security guys. Just pile on the mascara and get your legs out from under those bloody jeans.'

Mo stifled a sharp retort and put her foot on the accelerator. If working with Hayes had its sticky moments, that was the price to pay for jumping onto the Melrose Unit bandwagon instead of staying on her high horse at the SFO.

Hayes leapt out at the estate office, leaving his sergeant to cycle back to the Red Lion in the rain. Tough. Lights still glimmered in the incident room, Sunday night giving no quarter to Clarke's not-so-merry men. Hedgecoe was processing a pile of statements at the photocopier and the sexy-looking WPC he remembered seeing earlier was still beating the daylights out of the computer.

'Hi there, no day of rest for you then, Sergeant,' Hayes said with a chuckle. 'DI Clarke at the station?'

'Yes, sir, we've had a busy day with all the DNA volunteers. Thought it quite a lark some of 'em, though there were a few bad lads who were surprised to find themselves already on file.'

'Mr Wickham not included?'

'Not so far, and Superintendent Fox is not hopeful. An expensive waste of resources I reckon.'

'I agree. No matter, we'll catch the blighter in the end, just have to widen the net. I shall be in London tomorrow to meet Sir William. To maximize my efforts, any chance of looking up Lady Brigham's doctor's surgery? I assume she had a private physician.'

Hedgecoe frowned but could see no way of avoiding Hayes' direct assault. 'Yes, of course, sir. We've got it here.'

'Excellent.' Hayes followed Clarke's sidekick into the main office and watched him unlock a filing cabinet before finally producing a leather-bound address book.

Hayes whooped with delight, falling on the prize like an

eagle snatching up an unsuspecting mousie. Hedgecoe backed away, mumbling something about 'evidence' and looking decidedly anxious.

'It's OK, Sergeant, I'll get it back to you first thing in the morning. Mind if I use this office to make a few calls?'

Hedgecoe closed the door behind him and mouthed a foul expletive not lost on Wendy who, pausing in her attack on the keyboard, grinned. 'Fancy a coffee, Gary?'

'Hello, Maurice, it's Hayes here. I shall be calling in tomorrow to check a few points with Bennet. Did you get anywhere with that query of mine about the Match Point dating outfit? Thanks, chum.'

Trusting messages to an answerphone always left Hayes with misgivings akin to throwing a message in a bottle out to sea.

Twenty-One

Hayes fixed an appointment with Suzie Brigham's doctor for two thirty and checked the train timetable to coordinate a prompt arrival at the Lincoln's Inn chambers. After Prentice had driven off he spent a useful hour searching through Suzie's address book and checking entries against a list of known locals.

There wasn't much to go on and Suzie's God-awful handwriting didn't help. The woman further confused things by inserting initials or just given names in the appropriate alphabetical slots. The address book was well worn and, he decided, had probably come into use before her marriage if the proliferation of modelling agencies was any guide. He decided to hang on to this little treasure and test it out on her ex-husband, Fritz Grice, whose mobile number was conveniently listed. He phoned Fritz and got a dusty answer.

'What? Who did you say? Detective Superintendent Baines?'

'No, Hayes. H.A.Y.E.S.'

'Not another fucking break-in at my studio, surely?'

'No, it's about your former wife, Suzannah. I wonder if we could have a word?'

'Suzie? The poor cow *is* dead, isn't she?' His voice came across thickly, like a man emerging from a nightmare.

'Yes, I'm sorry, but I need to check all her contacts and you might be able to clarify a few problems here, Mr Grice. I would be extremely grateful if you could fit in a few minutes of your time today if that's possible, sir.'

'I'm booked on a shoot all day. At the V and A in South Kensington.'

'The museum?'

'Got it. I can't say when I'll be free but just barge in, though what help I can be to your investigation Christ knows. I haven't seen Suzie for weeks.'

He arrived at the solicitor's office with time to spare and whiled away a quarter of an hour exploring an area of London with which he was totally unfamiliar. The weather had done an about-turn, the autumn day as bright as a shower of gold, the trees in the square forming a glorious canopy. In contrast the solicitor's office, on the first floor of a magisterial building, was gloomy, the dust motes suspended in the morning light bravely filtering through the locked windows only emphasizing the staleness of the rooms.

'Mr Wainwright will see you now, Superintendent. Please follow me.'

Hayes buttoned his jacket and hoped this introduction to the sorrowing widower was not going to take on the air of a confrontation. But there were serious questions to ask. And did the man not appreciate the special protection he had already been given? An official umbrella to shelter an unimportant EU official from the intrusive winds of public interest? Why?

As he entered, the sober-looking character behind the desk rose and held out his hand, a welcoming gesture which softened a difficult situation. 'May I introduce Sir William, Superintendent?'

The other occupant remained glued to his chair, his broad back and bull-like neck unmoving. Hayes stepped forward to greet the seated figure whose head, wreathed in cigar smoke, nodded in grim acknowledgement of the tall, saturnine detective he had been warned about.

'Shall we get straight down to business, Superintendent?' Wainwright smoothly interjected. 'I believe you have some questions Sir William may be able to assist you with. Please take a seat.'

Hayes dropped onto a chair and pulled a file from his document case, letting an awkward silence develop while he studied his interviewee. Brigham was dressed formally, the smooth lapels of his Savile Row suit and crisply laundered shirt giving nothing away. Not so much as a black tie and the hooded eyes had, at a guess, shed no tears for many a year. The man watched Hayes with the unwinking gaze of a Buddha.

'I must first express my sympathy for your loss,' Hayes began. 'And, if you will allow me, perhaps you would be good enough to reiterate your movements prior to Lady Brigham's death.' Pen poised, Hayes waited for a reaction which came, as he expected, in a gruff response.

'I've already told everything to Clarke.'

'Yes, I appreciate that, Sir William, but Commander Crick, who, as you know, brought the Melrose Unit onto the scene, is insistent that the Met have an independent record.'

'A lot of bloody red tape if you ask me!'

Wainwright looked pained and murmured soothing assurances that prodded Brigham reluctantly to cooperate. Hayes persisted with the basic questions, noting with veiled amusement that Wainwright had, without so much as an apology, activated discreet recording equipment. The interview droned on and just when Brigham was settling into an acquiescent mood, Hayes struck.

'Tell me, Sir William, was your second marriage successful?'

He started up, a deep flush mottling his jowls. 'What bloody cheek! I've no intention of—'

Wainwright broke in with a flurry of apologies and Hayes continued.

'I regret the necessity to delve into your private life, Sir William, but this is a murder enquiry. Now, bearing in mind that you and Lady Brigham lived mainly separate lives either side of the Channel, would you say the relationship was harmonious?'

'Absolutely.'

'And it is not true that you intended to sell the Grange?'

'It had been mooted.'

'To live where?'

'We hadn't decided. Possibly in Ireland. I have business interests there.'

'Ah yes, the stud farm. Did your children know about

this, that the wedding would be the last family celebration at the old home and that the horses would go?'

'I had not discussed it with Zita.'

'But you discussed it in detail with your estate manager, Mr Wickham.'

'There was an understanding, yes, but nothing had been fixed.'

'What about the wedding reception at the house?'

'The arrangements must be cancelled,' he said with finality.

Hayes rather suspected this would be news to Eva and her mother but, having shaken the man from his initial belligerent response, he shaped up for a second round.

'The loss of your unborn child must have been a double blow.'

Brigham's face froze.

'You did know about the pregnancy, of course? I'm not breaking any confidence here, I hope? I only ask because when I mentioned the sad news to the ex-Lady Brigham she insisted that you decided twenty years ago that your family was complete. A surgical solution.'

'Zita's a bloody fool! And you can stop calling her Lady Brigham. I earned the title *after* my divorce, Zita has no right calling herself Lady Anything. Suzannah was the only Lady Brigham.'

This seemed something of a red herring, hardly of any importance in comparison with Brigham's other troubles. But, there again, perhaps to this bullyboy the title *was* important, and Zita's insistence on living nearby, and, in the process, embarrassing not only her ex-husband but half the county set who were as confused as Brigham's immediate neighbours by the family spat on their doorstep.

Despite indelicate probing Hayes got no further with Brigham on the pregnancy question and changed tack. 'Tell me, out of interest, Sir William, why did you suddenly leave Bluetex?'

Brigham relaxed. 'It was not a sudden departure, Superintendent. My wife – Suzannah – had serious misgivings about animal testing and before we married she insisted I sever my work in the pharmaceutical field.'

'She was an activist?'

'No, of course not. But she objected to the laboratory use of animals and was quite firm about it. My work with the EU is stimulating, and leaving England was not such a wrench, believe me.'

Wainwright insisted on bringing the interview to a swift conclusion and wound up the meeting with scant regard to protocol.

Hayes took a taxi to South Kensington and hoped his talk with Fritz Grice would progress on a lighter note. He alighted at the museum and was, after a brief discussion with the curator, steered to a cordoned-off area in the sculpture court where arc lights and raised voices set the scene for Grice's fashion shoot. But before he could settle down to enjoy the farcical operetta being played out against a backdrop of classical pillars and Roman heads, his cellphone broke through. A museum attendant rushed up. 'No mobiles!' he hissed, causing heads to swivel and focus on the interloper.

'Oh, sorry.' Hayes hurried out and found a side exit. 'Yes? What do you want, Prentice? I'm in a meeting, make it quick.'

'A breakthrough, sir. I've found the missing car.'

'What?'

'That red sports car Forensics have been looking for. It's an old MG. I spotted it in a supermarket car park here. I was getting a sandwich,' she added. 'Being curious I was peering inside and this bloke tapped me on the shoulder. Guess who it was?'

'For Christ's sake, Prentice, I said *be quick*.'

'He introduced himself, asked if I was interested in classic cars. A real charmer.'

'And?'

'It was Freddie MacCann. I didn't let on I was a police-woman.'

'You've reported it to Clarke?'

'Not yet, sir.'

'Well, get straight on to Clarke and make him chase it up immediately. Might not be linked to the evidence SOCO are sitting on but could be dynamite.'

'I checked the tyres, too. One's new and the other three are pretty worn like the police mechanic thought from the analysis of the tyre tracks.'

'Bingo!'

Twenty-Two

Hayes' talk with Grice turned out to be a stop-go discussion frequently interrupted by the exigencies of dressing the set. Stick-thin girls in pseudo-Grecian confections were pushed and pulled into place, their endurance a miracle of patience. He could only guess that the money made up for it.

An interview conducted under these constraints was a first for Hayes, for which his elevated powers as a detective superintendent investigating a murder counted for very little. Bemused by this new experience, he kept his cool and eventually had to admit that Fritz Grice's input had been helpful, not least because he phoned Daphne Solomon on the spot to introduce Hayes and persuade her to agree to Prentice's undercover mission at Match Point that evening.

'Daphne's an old mate of mine, this dating lark of hers is perfectly kosher, Hayes. There was a bit of a fuss over the infiltration of a coke dealer a year ago but Daph slung him out before the Drugs Squad got to hear of it. And, let's admit it, chum, picking off cocaine parties in Mayfair's low on the Met's agenda.'

When Hayes felt he had squeezed Grice as far as he would go, he made his farewells and sprinted to the exit, hailed a taxi and arrived at Doctor Azuri's consulting rooms with only minutes to spare. Suzie's gynaecologist occupied premises near Portland Place and he was admitted with no problem, but Hayes anticipated that the good doctor's response to police enquiries about a patient would be severely limited by professional discretion.

As it happened his pessimism was unwarranted. Azuri proved to be an affable guy, youthful, immaculately turned out in a grey suit and a cashmere polo neck but with the penetrating gaze of a cobra.

'It is very good of you to spare your time, Doctor Azuri.'

'Not at all, Superintendent. I doubt there can be anything I can add to your enquiries but Lady Brigham was a charming lady, her loss is a terrible tragedy.'

'She had been your patient for long?'

'Oh, indeed. For at least nine years, well before her recent marriage.'

'Not all that recent.'

'Really? You must be right. Time flies,' he said with a smile. His teeth were perfect, as white and even as Christmas card snow.

'Are you willing to help us?'

'As far as I am able. Cooperation with a police investigation is the least I can do for the poor woman.'

'The pregnancy is the problem,' Hayes admitted. 'Were you aware that Sir William allegedly underwent a vasectomy twenty years ago?'

'I have not had the pleasure of meeting Sir William, you will have to approach his own doctor on that score or ask the man directly.'

'Lady Brigham never mentioned such a thing?'

'Let's call her Miss Anstruther, shall we? As a patient of long standing she first consulted me as Suzannah Anstruther and we continued with this appellation as a sop to my secretary, who has difficulty with filing since our patients seem to have a confusing desire to use either their professional names or their newly acquired titles such as Madame This or the Duchess of That.'

Azuri grinned, inviting Hayes to share this little jibe, and it was clear that the man had reached the pinnacle of his profession not hamstrung by any lack of charm. The ladies must love him, Hayes decided, and plunged on in the hope that some useful information lay under the veneer of affability.

'Would you be willing to colour in some background, Doctor? For example, when did your medical association begin?'

'Miss Anstruther came to me with menstrual problems. Nothing serious, a side-effect of anorexia and drug abuse brought about by her desire to succeed as a top model. It's a punishing career.'

'The drug abuse was serious?'

'By the time she consulted me on her gynaecological ailments she had all but conquered the craving, and as far as I know stayed clean thereafter. She had the support of the man who became her first husband.'

'Fritz Grice.'

'Indeed. Mr Grice was instrumental in her complete recovery, and after the wedding, Suzie Anstruther, as I knew her, retired from the fashion scene. Regrettably, the marriage foundered, which, in my personal view, was a sad outcome. Mr Grice was a rock and Suzie's antics were, she later admitted to me, the result of boredom and a lack of self-esteem after ceasing to be regarded as a minor celebrity and losing the only job she was trained for. The final break-up came about after the miscarriage.'

Hayes started up. 'While she was with Grice?'

'Yes, there were complications I prefer not to go into but in my branch of medicine the psychological after-effects of such an accident can often exert an extraordinary change of character. To relieve her depression, my poor patient embarked on a rackety lifestyle only saved by a fortuitous introduction to riding. After the Grice divorce Sir William came on the scene and his powerful personality, allied to what turned out to be inflated claims of wealth, turned her head. The marriage was a disaster, in my opinion.'

'Her pregnancy? She consulted you, of course?'

Azuri frowned. 'My frankness will not be featured in any court proceedings, I trust?'

'Of course not,' Hayes assured him, crossing his fingers under the desk.

'Miss Anstruther wanted an abortion. Became hysterical, in fact, insisted her marriage to Brigham was at an end.'

'The baby was his?'

'We did not discuss paternity but, considering his age, I rather doubt it.'

'Suzie was not on any IVF track, then?'

'Absolutely not. Miss Anstruther was a healthy young woman with an initial anxiety about the pregnancy. I suggested counselling but she refused. A few weeks later she returned here and said she had decided to keep the baby. Her mood was euphoric. No explanation was given, she just changed her mind. Not unusual,' he said with a slight grimace, 'in such circumstances, especially since she had been affected so badly after the previous miscarriage.'

'A natural miscarriage?'

'Yes, I'm certain of that. At the time Miss Anstruther was not in the best of health but in recent years the riding had opened up an entirely new vista for her. Suzie Anstruther would have made a perfect mother and the scan was positive.'

Azuri rose and held out his hand in a polite indication that the interview was terminated. Hayes accepted the short straw and made a dignified departure, doing the decent thing by pausing to admire the bowl of roses on the secretary's desk in the outer office. The mature and actually unlovely PA was, at first glance, an odd choice for a smooth operator like Azuri, but perhaps his fashionable clientele could do without any competition on the glamour front, what with morning sickness or menopausal flushes dogging their flagging steps to his surgery.

Meeting up with Mo Prentice at the Pimlico headquarters later that afternoon brought him up short. His own assistant had transmogrified into a veritable Sloane, her hair now falling in loose waves about her shoulders, her long, long legs seductively enmeshed in fishnet stockings tucked into black suede boots.

'Very tasty,' Hayes admiringly remarked, aware of Maurice Gibson's grinning participation in mentally applauding the transformation of their oh so serious former Fraud Office interrogator.

'Let's pop out for a sandwich, Prentice. I missed my damned lunch yet again. There's a Starbucks up the road, you can fill me in on Clarke's reaction to your breakthrough with the MacCann vehicle.'

'He's been arrested on suspicion, sir. His DNA ties up with the semen specimen taken from the victim. Do you still want me to go on this undercover jaunt?'

'Might as well. Fritz Grice has set it up with the owner, Daphne Solomon. She's expecting you and, who knows, you might dig out more about naughty Freddie's antics at the dating agency. I'll take the car so you will be free to take your share of the champagne.'

'But I don't drink, sir.'

Hayes shrugged. 'Good for you. If you like you can stay overnight at your own place and get the train back to Horsham in the morning. Can't have you turning up for work in that gear, it'd give poor old Clarke entirely the wrong idea.'

Twenty-Three

Mo arrived at the Cuckoo Club just before five and was immediately taken by the doorman through to Daphne Solomon's office.

The proprietor of the Match Point dating agency was nervous and the appearance of this attractive young investigator was something she wished now she had not been persuaded to participate in. Mo produced her ID and waited while it was carefully scrutinized.

'Miss Prentice. Please sit down, we need to talk.'

Daphne Solomon, fiftyish, presented a youthful figure well honed by Renton's exercise routine. Her hair was glossy as a shampoo ad and even the tinted specs she wore in no way diminished an understated glamour which set her apart from the image Mo had envisioned: a cross between a dance hostess and a traditional marriage-broker. Mo dropped into a leather armchair, adjusting her skirt and crossing her legs in a relaxed pose she was far from feeling.

'I only agreed to this arrangement because I trust Fritz,' she said, her voice modulated to a throaty undertone. Mo suspected the sexy timbre was the product of a lifetime's smoking but had to admit it sounded classy. 'Before I let you join our little party, Miss Prentice, perhaps you could elaborate on your reason for coming here.'

'Oh, please call me Mo,' she said, fixing Daphne Solomon with serious intent. 'As Mr Grice probably explained, my work with the Met is in a minor capacity, part of a team effort to flush out one or two individuals who have been causing problems, in a nutshell making nuisances of themselves stalking women they meet either on the Internet or through dating agencies.'

'And this special unit is?'

'The Melrose Unit.'

'Should I have heard of this Melrose outfit?'

'We try to keep a low profile, Mrs Solomon, but many victims of these men have been traumatized by persistent nuisance calls at home, stalking and threats. In one instance, there was blackmail . . .' She paused, noting that Solomon's attention had sharpened. 'It is a nasty business and anything you can do to help track down any of these sexual predators would be beneficial to your business and very much appreciated by the police.'

'Do you suspect someone who is a member here? I could let you see a membership list if you gave me your professional assurance that the names would be given the strictest confidence.'

'That would be useful.'

'This is a very exclusive club, you realize. I take pains to verify applicants and the Association of British Introduction Agencies backs up our stringent security efforts,' she said, offering Mo a cigarette from an onyx box. 'Do you smoke?'

'Not just now, thank you. Are you quite sure none of your clients has experienced problems with dates?'

'None.'

'Good. If I might mingle informally, introduce myself and test the water, one visit will, I'm sure, be adequate scrutiny and we can assure you that your business is safeguarded. No problems with illegal substances as far as you are aware, Mrs Solomon?'

Her mouth pursed in an ugly moue which caused hairline cracks to appear in the perfect maquillage. 'Certainly not,' she snapped, rising to her feet and giving Mo a penetrating reappraisal before crossing to a locked filing cabinet and extracting a photocopy of the membership list. She held the sheet in her hand and regarded Mo over her dark glasses. 'Look, Miss Prentice, I'm not totally happy with a police presence but if you behave yourself and cause no embarrassment to my clients, an hour of your time will be acceptable.' Mo took the list and swiftly folded it out of sight in her clutch bag.

Mrs Solomon stood, suddenly uncertain whether Fritz Grice's assurances were good enough. 'Do you have any names for these stalkers, photofits, anything useful?'

'These people are very devious and joining an agency under a false name is not, you must admit, unknown.'

Daphne Solomon stiffened and Mo felt a chill breeze waft away what she had hoped had been a reassuring interview. In truth Mo felt uncomfortable with this undercover lark, awkward with the smooth lies she had found herself mouthing to a person who, on the face of it, was only offering an opportunity for lonely people to meet like-minded souls.

'One last question if I may, Mrs Solomon,' she said, pausing with her hand firmly against the door. 'Do you find it easy to balance the intake? I would have thought women would be more likely to be attracted to Match Point.'

Daphne Solomon touched her immaculate coiffure with heavily ringed fingers. 'It's an art,' she said with a nervous laugh. 'A trade secret, Miss Prentice. Now, let me introduce you to one or two of my nice guests.'

The next hour passed pleasantly enough and Mo relaxed. Maybe this security game wasn't so bad after all. She sipped her tonic water and dipped into the canapés and cocktail nibbles circulated by a pair of robotic waiters, finding the company fascinating. The ladies were, on the whole, older than Mo and her appearance as a new client attracted the eager attention of several business types in suits. It had apparently been unnecessary for young bloods such as Renton or Freddie MacCann to be wheeled out tonight and the party atmosphere, augmented by the muted background rhythms of a jazz trio, was far from threatening. Mo, losing her anxiety about her invidious infiltration of a nice bunch of people, even found herself having fun.

Towards seven the pairing off became slightly desperate and Mo withdrew to the ladies' room to escape the attentions of a determined bloke with red hair and halitosis.

One other stood in front of the long mirror renewing her lipstick, an elegant woman exuding a powerful aroma of Poison. 'Hi, you must be new here, I've been abroad for a few months. My name's Judy. Had any luck?'

Mo smiled. 'Not so you'd notice. I've been coming on and off since Christmas but nothing's turned up so far.'

'Who introduced you?'

'My personal trainer.'

'Not Renny Brigham!'

'Yes, how did you guess?'

Judy laughed. 'Renny's Daphne's one-man publicity machine. Moves in all the right circles and can be relied on to turn up with a hunk if Daphne's worried. Opportunities to meet people have to be engineered these days and middle-aged men can be bloody picky. Any girl looking for a serious relationship can get urgent. Take my advice, it's much better to party without any romantic notions, just enjoy the dates and keep circulating. You're a bit young for a place like this, if I may say so. On the rebound, sweetie?'

'Er, yes, sort of. Renny thought it would take me out of myself and when I came before I met this smashing guy called Frederick.'

'Freddie MacCann?'

'You know him?'

'I know everyone here, ducky. It gets quite boring seeing the same old faces week in and week out. But I've been in the States for a while and this evening I had nothing better to do and it seemed like a laugh to catch up on the regulars. Freddie's a fixture here. Desperate Dan, I call him.'

'Why's that? I thought he was absolutely lovely.'

'On the make, lovie. Like all the dishy types. You keep clear of blokes like that, poor as they come, and only looking for a handout. They don't even go dutch on a dinner date, but worth every penny if you're not heartbroken. Did he ever tell you what he did for a living?'

'He's an antiques dealer.'

Judy let out an unladylike snort and leaned against the basin choking with delight.

'He told you *that*? Mind you, I got the same line myself but, by the merest chance, I spotted our Fred at Chester's, you know, that big auction house in Wyndhams Mews.'

'He was bidding?'

'No, holding up a Chagall sketch. The place was packed out with Russian nouveaux and I had tagged along with a French friend of mine who was new to the art game. Could have knocked me sideways seeing Freddie up there in his warehouseman's overall.'

'Well, he *did* make it in the end, Judy. He's got himself a shop in Sussex and he's to be married to a girl I knew at school.'

'Rich, is she?'

'Her father is.'

'Bet he put up the dosh, then. When I last saw Freddie MacCann he hadn't a bean.'

Mo nervously brushed her skirt and stepped back. 'I'd better be going, Judy. See you around?'

'Not here, worse luck. My old man got wind of my little excursions, put a tail on me, the rotten sod. I'm back to home ground after tomorrow when he gets back from Texas. Promised to be on my good behaviour.'

'You're married?'

'Sure. Don't look so shocked, girl, half the women here are well and truly wedded. They just pop along to Daphne's to meet men, do a few lunch dates and relieve the boredom of living in suburbia.'

'The men too?'

'A good proportion, I'd guess.'

Mo looked aghast. 'But that destroys the whole concept, doesn't it? I thought this was a sort of matrimonial agency, a place for singles.'

'Listen, honey, the moment you start twittering about wedding bells and babies we'll all be crushed underfoot in the rush of bastards making for the exit. Don't take it seriously, sweetheart. Match Point is just a launch pad, Daphne's not expecting to lose half her membership at the altar rails.'

Mo grabbed a taxi and had a shower as soon as she got home. It was all so bloody cynical. Whatever happened to true love? But after microwaving a pizza and settling down with a steaming pot of coffee she felt better and braced herself to make some notes on this abortive sally into the

Mayfair breeding haunts. She recovered the Match Point membership list from her bag and settled down for a browse. It was a pity she missed Suzie's name, it was to take old clever socks, Hayes, to point out that Anstruther was the one that should have rung the alarm bells.

Twenty-Four

After phoning Hayes to give him the low-down on her jaunt, Mo relaxed for an unforeseen evening at home while Hayes, fired up by the chase, made like an arrow for the Horsham nick. Clarke waylaid him at the door and steered his unwanted co-investigator into a back room furnished with filing cabinets and two broken chairs.

'What's the game, Clarke?'

'Thought we'd better have a private word before the Superintendent muscles in.'

'You're holding MacCann on suspicion?'

'That's the ticket.'

'My sergeant found the MG for you.'

'A lucky strike.'

'If you say so. What's the story?'

'Refuses to say anything till his solicitor gets here, which should be any minute now. The DNA puts the slimy devil in the frame, no messing. We brought the car in and the forensic boss swears the paint samples match. But we haven't got a firm link with the tyre moulds taken from the crime scene yet.' Clarke grinned. 'Good enough, though. Looks like it's all tied up. The quickest snatch I've been involved in.'

'I will be in on the interview.'

'Well, I'll have to confirm that, sir.'

Hayes' eyes narrowed. 'As the senior ranking officer here I'm setting the rules, OK?'

Clarke shrugged. 'How did your girl get on in London?'

Hayes looked surprised. 'You heard about that?'

'Nobody goes undercover in this investigation without

someone picking it up.' Clarke made the score even, one point each. Hayes let it go.

'Prentice did well. She looks the part, can do "classy" and is an experienced officer. I spoke to her on the phone on my way down. She got a general idea of the Match Point set-up and picked up a few pointers but it adds little to the case against MacCann except there was an impression that the guy was looking for a meal ticket. Less than a year ago he was employed as a warehouseman at a top auction house. Leasing a shop and stocking it with antiques was a big jump. Could he have been approached by a fence looking for a quiet backwater where he could dump some iffy stuff? Any ideas?'

'MacCann says he has a business partner.'

Hayes whistled. 'You don't say! Who's the lucky man? You've seen his accounts?'

'I made a request to his bank manager but he won't pass on any details until he has the go-ahead from head office.'

'But our lad wouldn't name his backer?'

'Clammed up. It only came out because we checked the purchase of the van. A local dealer confirmed that it was paid for by a buyer who wished to remain anonymous but registered the van in MacCann's name.'

'A woman?'

Clarke shrugged. 'We shall just have to wait till his brief turns up. He reckons once the lawyer gets here he'll be released.'

Hayes leaned against the wall and lit a cigarette, regarding Clarke with a distinct lack of confidence. The man looked exhausted, his shirt collar crumpled like a concertina, his eyes bloodshot. 'Seems to me, Inspector, you've got a thin case here, mate. The guy has a thing going with his prospective father-in-law's wife the night she's killed but shoots off smartish and presumably says he left her in the pink. Does he have a witness to vouch for the time he left? The only thing he admits is having a financial backer for his antiques business. Hardly unknown, is it? In MacCann's job at Chester's he must have made a lot of useful contacts in the trade, and if a punter wanted to invest in a promising venture fronted by a chap with bags of charm and a flair for the business, it hardly fits up our suspect on a murder charge.'

'You're not allowed to smoke in here,' Clarke muttered. His mobile rang and he turned aside to take the call, lowering his voice to an undertone.

'That was Superintendent Fox. He's tied up at a retirement do in Brighton but wants a full report before we leave MacCann to stew in a cell overnight.'

'Tricky. Let's hope the solicitor puts his skates on, then. You're not intending to let this bird fly are you, Clarke?'

Fortunately a knock on the door precluded the DI's sharp rejoinder and a WPC entered to announce the arrival of MacCann's brief. 'A Mr Macey, sir. He's waiting at the desk. He left this,' she said, handing Clarke a business card.

Hayes glanced at his watch. Nearly nine thirty and the chances were MacCann would walk before midnight. He stubbed out his cigarette and strode ahead, leaving Clarke to scramble in his wake with the WPC in close formation. They made an odd procession: the tall figure of Hayes taking giant strides dogged by the middle-aged and comfortably rounded DI Clarke, followed by the maid of honour, the delectable Wendy who was such a whiz on the incident-room computer.

Gerald Macey looked well able to snatch his client from any loosely constructed charge and presented a smoothly suited persona impatiently tapping his gold biro on the duty sergeant's counter. He held out his hand. 'You must be DI Clarke,' he said.

'No. I am Detective Superintendent Hayes from the Met and I have been drafted down here to cover this investigation.'

Macey's aplomb ducked from this unexpected bouncer but quickly recovered as Clarke introduced himself.

'Shall we get this over with, gentlemen? My client has already been held here on a trumped-up charge for several hours, and I'm sure any misunderstanding can be immediately corrected.'

Clarke proceeded to bluster his way through an indictment

only brought to a halt by Hayes' demand that MacCann was transferred to an interview room without further delay. Macey got the message and attached himself firmly to the senior man, leaving Clarke to muster his troops via the duty sergeant.

Twenty-Five

The windowless interview room was lit by megawatt downlighters, giving MacCann's face a greenish tinge which washed out the healthy glow of his good looks. The man looked drained, his nervousness accentuated by a throbbing pulse at his temple.

Hayes quickly took a seat, Clarke plumping himself down on his right opposite the suspect. The solicitor, Macey, opened a legal pad on the table, and regarded the two officers with curiosity.

He was familiar with such interview cells, the majority of his clients being from the minor criminal classes, but the presence of a senior Met officer was a facer.

What was the subplot in all this? Presumably the intervention of Sir William Brigham was the key, though why the widower would hasten to pull in an expensive legal firm to protect his wife's suspected murderer was a problem he had not yet had a chance to unravel. His initial talk with Frederick MacCann had been brief but the evidence seemed thin, and his advice to his client was clear: 'Remember you are innocent and commit yourself only to covering the basic facts. If you are asked questions which I think may incriminate you, I shall intervene. Trust me, Mr MacCann, and we shall have you out of here without a stain on your character.'

Clarke took the initiative and brought the recording equipment into play. He spoke first, and after putting the preliminary questions, jumped straight in.

'Shall we start with a statement regarding your visit to Aspern Grange on the evening of Wednesday October 12th? You do not dispute your liaison with Lady Brigham, I presume?'

MacCann glanced at Macey, who gave a curt nod, and then cleared his throat before putting his case.

'I arrived about nine.'

'You were expected?'

'Suzie left a note at the shop with my assistant. I was out at a country-house auction in Hassocks.'

'You kept the note?' Hayes broke in.

'No, of course not. Suzie was married, she wouldn't want anything like that left lying about. I burnt it.'

'Sorry. Please continue.'

'We had been meeting for months, ever since Easter on and off. We first met at a place in town where I used to go.'

Hayes raised an eyebrow. 'The Cuckoo Club?'

'Yeah, you know it?'

'Not personally, but my sergeant has been to Match Point, which is where you were introduced to your fiancée, I gather.'

'Eva. Yes, that's right. But I already knew Suzie before Renny brought his sister along.'

'Renton Brigham knew his stepmother went to the club?'

'Sure. It was Renton who told her about it. Suzie was intrigued and dropped in a few times out of curiosity. It's only a private drinking club really, nothing heavy. We hit it off straight away.'

'Then you met Eva.'

MacCann closed his eyes as if the exact recollection of the sequence of events was a problem. After a moment or two's silence Hayes prompted a reply, raising a warning hand to Macey who moved to interrupt. 'This is a serious matter, Mr MacCann,' Hayes said firmly, 'and your co-operation would be helpful to your situation here.'

'OK, I admit seeing Suzie at the Grange and sometimes at her place in Notting Hill before I knew Eva. Renny introduced me and at first it was just a bit of fun, stringing the two of them along. Suzie had a wicked streak, you see, it amused her knowing I was suddenly the flavour of the month with her husband because of Eva.'

'How so?'

'Eva made no secret of wanting to get married. At the time I only had that lousy job at Chester's, there was no way I was going to go down that road even if I'd wanted to. Suzie and I had fallen in love, head over heels, it wasn't just a fling, but then Brigham asked me over to his London house and, you can take it from me, I really got the shits, thought Renny had shopped me over my affair with Suzie.'

'But you had been discreet?'

'It was difficult. Wickham was always nosing about the place, checking the stables late at night after he got back from the pub, and he was in the old man's pocket so we had to be extra careful. But with no staff living in and Brigham abroad most of the time we had a pretty clear run of it.'

'Then Eva came along.'

MacCann bit his lip. 'Yeah. Nice kid but not really my type, too pushy. I could see her shaping up to a re-run of Zita in twenty years' time.'

'But you proposed. Was that Suzie's idea?'

'Suzie? No way. Like I said her old man asked me over to the Notting Hill pad he keeps for overnights but as it turned out it wasn't a showdown about Suzie.' He laughed. 'The silly old sod wanted to cake me up. Offered a quarter of a million, yeah, quite a bung, wasn't it, Inspector Clarke?'

'To leave Suzie alone?'

'No, he didn't know about us. He wanted to set me up in business to give me a better chance with Zita. Eva wanted to marry me but her ma wasn't having her hitched to a bloody pauper. William had fallen out with Eva after the divorce and he hoped that bringing me into the family with a respectable business behind me would also sweeten Zita. And he was right, wasn't he? Don't look so po-faced, Superintendent, it was an offer I couldn't refuse as they say, my only chance of jumping on the ladder.'

'But you love Eva?'

He shrugged. 'Yeah, but not like I loved Suzie.' His eyes, Clarke was surprised to notice, suddenly welled up.

Macey coughed. 'Perhaps my client would like a break.'

But Frederick blew his nose and insisted on continuing.

Clarke kicked off. 'Did you know that Lady Brigham was pregnant?'

He nodded. 'She said she'd get rid of it at first but changed her mind after a big blow-up with William.'

'He guessed it wasn't his child?'

'No, he never found out about it.'

'Well, he knows now. The pathologist told him.'

'Christ!'

'I have spoken with Doctor Azuri,' Hayes put in. 'He tells me that Suzie was entirely happy with her pregnancy. There was no question of it being your baby? She wasn't threatening you with a paternity suit or exposure to her husband?'

'No, of course not. The thing was the engagement had been in the papers, wedding invites sent out, the whole shebang. Suzie got William to agree to a no-fault divorce. The old guy wasn't as rich as she'd thought and the country life had become difficult for her after the pony-club idea folded. You heard about that? The Kipling kid getting killed?'

Hayes nodded. 'Yes, go on, you were saying Suzie hoped to split amicably and get out before the pregnancy became obvious?'

'The arrangement was she would accept a lump sum as a final settlement which would also include the Notting Hill property. The announcement of their divorce would be delayed until after the wedding but Suzie had decided to go abroad before Christmas. She reckoned the wedding would go smoother if she was diplomatically off the scene. It was to be Zita's show. Trouble was Brigham had racked up a pile of gambling debts at the races and needed to sell the Grange and retrench.'

'Not a situation diminished by entering into a financial arrangement with you, eh? Did Sir William retain a partnership in your shop?'

'No, it was an outright gift, a wedding present for Eva really.'

'Lucky girl. How did Renton take this favouritism?'

'Oh, Renny got his share in other ways.'

Clarke looked worried. 'This is all very neat, Mr MacCann, but, frankly, I don't buy it. From my experience, giving a new acquaintance a quarter of a million pounds with no strings attached sounds very unlike an astute businessman like Sir William Brigham. In my cynical view, a more likely scenario would be that you were paid to dispose of his wife before a very expensive second divorce finally cleaned him out. Why else would he employ a top legal brain like Mr Macey here to get you off the hook?'

MacCann visibly paled. 'Kill Suzie? Me a hit man for Brigham? You're fucking raving,' he said, jumping to his feet. Macey grabbed his arm and whispered an inaudible remonstration which Hayes insisted he repeat for the benefit of the recording.

'I think we shall leave now,' Macey insisted.

'Hang on, we've not finished,' Hayes said. 'Your client has only given us the barest facts about his movements on the night in question. Shall we pick it up from his stated arrival at the house?'

MacCann's hands trembled, his confidence now shot. The lawyer pushed a carafe towards him across the table and, after pouring a glass of water for his client, MacCann lit a cigarette and made a solid effort to recover his cool.

'You arrived at the Grange about nine,' Hayes prompted. 'Parked the MG in the coppice and Suzie let you into the house. OK so far?'

MacCann drew deeply on his cigarette and picked up the story. 'That's right. She was in great spirits. I suspected she had been having a sniff to hype herself up.'

'Cocaine?'

He nodded. 'Suzie wasn't hooked. She just liked a line of marching powder to put her in the party mood. We made love and afterwards we talked about her plans. She told me Wickham was taking the horses to Ireland next month.'

'She didn't mind that?'

'It was all part of the scaling-down of the estate before William put it on the market in the New Year. It was all very hush-hush, Zita was not to know about the divorce or the house sale. She would have done her nut, still thinks of it as her home, and given the chance would want to move back in or claim a share of the sale price I wouldn't wonder. Zita's a greedy cow and still considers herself the lady of the manor. Suzie didn't stand a chance here from the start. Only William and I were in on it, though a rumour about Eva's horse, Denzil, being sent off to the stud farm was going the rounds but that was the least of it.'

'Tell me, why did you keep the sports car under wraps?'

MacCann smiled, his eyes briefly lighting up. 'Oh, it was my little secret. I called it Rita, like Rita Hayworth, that old movie star with the red hair. That was what attracted me to Suzie first off – her red hair. I've had the MG for years, clung to it even when I was down on my uppers, and a mate of mine let me share his lock-up out at Gatwick. After I got the van, Rita came in useful on buying trips: gave the right impression, see, no one expects a dealer to roll up in a beat-up old banger. But the van was too obvious to use when I dropped in on Suzie so I'd kept quiet about Rita to everyone apart from Suzie and the girl who works in the shop when I'm not there.'

He stubbed out his cigarette and collected his thoughts. 'It was pissing down that night and dark as hell. We had a wonderful time – as I told you Suzie was pretty high before I even got there and she taught me a few things in bed which would make your brain turn somersaults. Afterwards we shared a bite to eat, souvlaki, before I pushed off about eleven but as I was pulling away I caught sight of this woman pedalling up the drive. I'm sure she didn't see me, she wore a hooded mac and had her head down because of the rain, but I drove off at a good lick and went back to the lock-up to swap Rita for the van before returning to the shop.'

'Did you recognize the cyclist?'

'I didn't stop, but there's only one nosey old bag who hangs about the estate at night. Wickham had warned Suzie about her but she pooh-poohed the idea. It was her cottage, you see. Wickham had seen her a few times creeping back after dark thinking no one guessed that she'd kept the spare keys.'

'A staff cottage?'

'Cosham's old place. I reckon the one I clocked that night could only have been that vicious old housekeeper of Suzie's. She was the one who hated Suzie enough to beat her brains out and Suzie should have taken notice of Wickham. I was there that night, Inspector Clarke, I'm not denying it, but I wasn't the last one out on the quiet.'

'And you are quite sure you closed the door when you left?'

'Suzie came downstairs to see me out and I heard her lock up. Whoever killed Suzie must have broken in while we were upstairs or else was already hidden in the house.'

Twenty-Six

Hayes turned to Macey. 'We shall have to postpone this interview, sir. It is important that we check out your client's statement before we continue.'

'He is released?'

'Unfortunately not tonight. We have yet to corroborate his claim that Mrs Cosham was a witness to him leaving and confirm the time of his departure. The time of death is a crucial factor.'

MacCann rose up, his face suffused with anger. 'You can't lock me up all night! I've told you the truth, man. I didn't kill Suzie!'

Macey addressed Clarke directly. 'Are you suggesting, Inspector, that my client is the prime suspect?'

'Until we find evidence to the contrary, yes, sir. I am not convinced that Mr MacCann has told us the full story with regard to his financial arrangement with Sir William, for a start.'

'I shall speak with Sir William myself,' Hayes insisted. It dawned on him that being brought in to safeguard Brigham's reputation was turning out a bum deal. Bennet had more on Brigham than he let on. Did they know the man had a reputation for gambling? Connections with shady characters in the racing game who may have persuaded him that the simplest way of solving his money problems was to put out a contract on his new wife, preferably an amateur, someone like MacCann who could be paid off on the apparently legitimate excuse of being a dowry for his estranged daughter? If that could be proved, Brigham was a devious bastard with more brains than Hayes had given him credit for.

Macey made a strong appeal to Clarke to allow MacCann bail, a plea which fell on deaf ears, and after a final show-down the solicitor left with only a morsel of hope that further police enquiries could only benefit his client.

Freddie MacCann was taken back to the cells while Clarke and Hayes repaired to his office to discuss their next move.

'I must have another go at Sir William. My boss will back me up, so he won't be able to dodge the issue like before,' Hayes grimly remarked.

'He's due back here tomorrow to make arrangements for the funeral, though I can't see the coroner releasing the body any earlier on the say-so of a local bigwig like Brigham stamping round.'

'Good. Any special points you want to clear up with him, Clarke? I'm not trying to whitewash the fellow but, as you know, I was only moved in on this case because the man has connections.'

'Connections?'

'Don't ask! I'm not fully in the picture myself on that score, but Brigham has powerful friends who insist we see fair play.'

'Fair play!' Clarke looked thunderous, his determination to keep on good terms with this bloke from the Met, a senior officer no less, all but shot to pieces. He had made discreet enquiries about this Melrose Unit: a new outfit responsible for hostage negotiation and witness and jury protection comprising experienced officers with, if his infor-mation rang true, an ability to bend the rules.

Hayes shrugged. 'Look, Inspector, I'm no pushover, believe me. If I can prove Brigham set MacCann up on this I shall have no hesitation putting it on record. Let's not fall out over this. I'll talk to Brigham while you check up on the locals. Wickham's not exactly in the clear, is he? And he's been a loyal servant of Brigham's for years, and a rough character to boot. A man more likely to have been persuaded to top Suzie than MacCann, who, in my book, is no better than an amateur gigolo.'

'What about the housekeeper, Cosham? She could turn out to be a useful witness. Shall I tackle her?'

Hayes drummed his fingers on the desk and mentally charted the best way of proceeding at this delicate point of the investigation.

'Cosham's a prickly sort, liable to clam up when she finds out we're on to her little excursions to the staff cottage at night. Wickham was told to turn a blind eye but once the police bring her in for questioning her attitude might turn nasty. May I suggest that you tackle the estate manager, and I insist on an informal interview with Brigham at the house without his solicitor present if possible, and we leave Cosham to my sergeant.'

Clarke stiffened. 'What? That tall girl?'

Hayes nodded. 'Prentice is known to Cosham. And an awkward customer with issues about her long service at the Grange would, at a guess, be contemptuous of a young female officer and relax under questioning. We have to play Cosham carefully, Clarke. If she denies being on the estate Wednesday night that's MacCann's alibi up the spout.'

'The pathologist's estimated time of death is that accurate?'

'No, of course not. But he reckons the victim was attacked no earlier than eleven and no later than three in the morning.'

'Doctor Harris is a bloody good man and solid as a rock on the witness stand. But we've only got MacCann's word for it that he left when he said he did. One thing ties up though. That souvlaki they had – some sort of Greek meat and pitta-bread sandwich, apparently: any chance of the pathologist pinning that down timewise from his analysis of the stomach contents and the rate of digestion?'

Hayes frowned. 'Probably. It must be in the autopsy report. But I'll leave you to handle that, I'm more interested in Brigham's association with MacCann. Would he really set the guy up in business just to get Eva married off?'

'It wasn't just that. According to MacCann it was a move to get back on fatherly terms with his daughter who had fallen for this useless bugger and needed to sweeten the pill to persuade Zita to approve of the marriage.'

'That girl's no teenager, Clarke! And she lives an independent life in London. It's not the Middle Ages, chum.'

'Don't you believe it. From local chit-chat the view is

she's still under Zita's thumb and getting married is her best chance of breaking away.'

'Does her mother have money?'

Clarke shrugged. 'Must have made a bundle in the past before she left the operatic scene. But if she does have a healthy bank balance she doesn't splash it about the village.'

Hayes stubbed out his cigarette and looked up. 'Are we agreed, then? You and your men scout round the village and put Wickham through the mincer about the deal with Sir William and his promotion with the Irish stud-farm relocation while I make myself pleasant to Sir William.'

'And Cosham?'

'Frankly, Cosham's small fry. Leave her to Sergeant Prentice. The best we're likely to get out of her is a vague admission of being in the vicinity late on Wednesday night. A woman riding a pushbike after dark in pouring rain would be a lousy witness even if she agreed to being there at all.'

Twenty-Seven

Mo Prentice was sitting in the public bar chatting to an elderly man wearing a tweed jacket with leather patches. Hayes breezed in and ordered a pint and she hurriedly excused herself from her grey-haired companion and followed him up to the bar.

'Who was that?'

'The churchwarden. Mr Henlowe.' She glanced at her watch. 'Gosh, I didn't realize how late it was. You missed dinner again, sir,' she said with a grin. 'If you weren't so skinny, Superintendent, I'd think you were on a diet.'

Hayes was in no mood for banter. 'No chance. You didn't wait, did you? Me, I'm stuck trying to get some sort of sensible agenda worked out with Clarke.'

'MacCann still in the frame?'

'Clarke's convinced he did it but I'm not so sure. But MacCann was the last man at the scene we've been able to pin down so far. Let's move into the back room, I'll get some sandwiches sent through and we'll compare notes. You sure you've eaten?'

They adjourned to the publican's private bolt-hole and Hayes lit up, his staccato movements warning Prentice to play it straight. The fire in the grate had long since expired and the closed-in atmosphere only intensified the air of suspense.

He was worried. Nothing seemed to add up. Wickham had walked into the house and found the body, so presumably the front door had been unlocked after MacCann's departure if what he said was true. Or Wickham had keys. MacCann was an amateur baddie for sure and if he *had* been hired to top Suzie, shooting off in a panic afterwards and slamming his MG into a tree would be in character and not closing the door properly behind him would have been par for the course.

'Now, Prentice, tell me, did you get anything from Tracey about Wickham's movements on Wednesday night?'

'She stuck to his story, sir. Said he got in about half eleven after the pub closed and didn't leave till next morning. Tracey's a poor liar in my opinion and sticking up for her man wouldn't extend to protecting him from suspicions about an affair with Suzie.'

'You reckon?'

'Can't see Wickham chancing his arm with the boss's wife, can you? In a place like this everyone watches the staff and a sexy guy like Bill Wickham would be the focus for any sort of innuendo.'

'But he would be regarded as an attractive stud from any woman's angle, eh?'

Prentice sipped her Coke and grew pensive. 'Yeah, sure, sir. And he scrubs up like a pro once he's in the saddle. If anyone was tempted, I'd put my money on Eva.'

Hayes polished off the round of sandwiches and lit another cigarette. Being hamstrung with this inexperienced detective sergeant was probably the best he could hope for when it came to support. Clarke was defensive of his own position in what was, in all likelihood, the key investigation of his entire career. 'Clarke's having a go at Wickham himself in the morning. I've got another line of enquiry for you, Prentice. Mrs Cosham.'

Hayes went over MacCann's testimony in detail and suggested the line of attack Mo should pursue. 'We need Cosham to commit to seeing MacCann's MG shoot off about midnight.'

She blew out her cheeks in dismay. 'She's not going to do that at this stage is she, sir? If she *was* cycling past the crime scene on Wednesday night she would have said so before. She's not the sort to miss a trick like that.'

'Ah, but she wasn't aware that her secret return visits to her old cottage had been seen and certainly didn't want to give the game away unless push came to shove. Getting the bloody woman to admit to roaming round that night is a long shot but it's all MacCann can come up with so we've got to follow it up. If you set the woman off on loose talk she might surprise us with something useful. No need to bring MacCann into the equation, just lead her in the right direction after you've told her that Wickham knew all about her little excursions and Suzie had said to let it go.'

'Wickham saw her, had followed her before, you mean?'

'According to MacCann, Suzie didn't much care and told Wickham to keep quiet about it. Maybe she was saving it up to add to a list of reasons to get rid of Cosham once and for all.'

'And if the housekeeper had spare keys for the staff cottages she must have had keys to the big house too . . .' The dark scenario this fact presented hung between them like a ghost.

Hayes rallied. 'Well, that's a whole new ball game, Prentice. Let's just concentrate on the things the woman *is* likely to admit to under your cunningly naive questioning.' He laughed. The whole bloody case was bizarre and tiptoeing round Clarke's bunch of rural plods was the least of it. After a few desultory exchanges about MacCann's chances, they called it a day.

He had arranged with Brigham's secretary to meet him at the house at twelve thirty. 'I'll push off back to the mortuary first thing and put some detailed queries before our eminent pathologist,' he said, catching Mo next morning in the process of mounting her bike after an early wake-up call. 'You've had breakfast?'

'No. I thought I'd better catch Mrs Cosham before she leaves for work. She's got a spring-cleaning party on the go at the Grange and I suspect she'll be more forthcoming without her domestics eyeing us up.'

Autumn sunshine glittered in the misty air, the sound of birdsong clamorous as church bells. Mo arrived at May Cripps' cottage just after eight and found Cissie Cosham and her sister still at breakfast. May had the look of one who had endured a poor night, her hair still netted and the

pink quilted dressing gown hanging loosely over a flannel-
ette nightie.

'Oh, my Lord, you've caught me in me curlers,' she said
with a giggle.

Cosham looked on stonily, remaining seated, her eyes
narrowing with suspicion. 'You're an early bird, Sergeant
Prentice. I suppose May and I must be the worms.'

Twenty-Eight

Cissie Cosham poured herself a second cup and tensely enquired, 'Now what can I do for you, Sergeant? I can only spare ten minutes, I have staff waiting for me at the Grange.'

May moved in to invite their guest to join them at the breakfast table. The room was not cluttered as the sitting room had been, and sunshine sparkled on a row of horse brasses nailed to the low beam overhead. Mo dumped her backpack on the floor and smiled brightly, accepting the cup of tea May offered with thanks. The two women stared expectantly and, for just a moment, Mo was lost for words.

'Er – well, yes. Mrs Cosham, it's a delicate matter. A question of your use of a staff cottage on the Brigham estate.'

May flushed, her anxious glance darting from her sister to the polite young policewoman sitting at their table.

Cissie's mouth gathered into a knot of irritation. 'I don't know what you mean,' she said flatly.

'It's a perfectly simple question, Mrs Cosham. You have been living here in Bluebell Cottage for approximately two years but, according to my information, continue to use a staff cottage.'

'Of course I do. Someone has to keep it clean, don't they? You can't leave a place empty for years on end.' She paused. 'Anyway I expect to move back in in due course, some of my things are still stored there. It was, in case your nosey informant failed to mention it, my home for over twenty years.'

'And you intend to return?'

'As soon as Sir William sees sense,' she snapped. 'No

point in me being miles down the road while the place gathers dust for no good reason.'

'Does Sir William know you have been using the cottage? Stayed overnight on occasions?' This was, Mo had to admit, a shot in the dark.

May half rose from her seat, her face a map of misery. 'That's my fault, miss. I snore you see, something terrible. It's my sinuses, the doctor reckons. Poor Cissie can't rest after I've taken a sleeping pill which makes my snoring worse than ever, she says.'

Cosham threw down her napkin. 'Just shut up, May, it's none of your business. Why don't you go upstairs and get dressed while I explain to the sergeant here?'

Like a whipped dog, May shuffled off, closing the latch with a gentle click as she left. Mo felt a stab of sympathy for these two, clamped together under one roof for no good reason other than Suzie Brigham's pique. Bluebell Cottage presumably had belonged to the younger woman, whose peaceful home had been invaded not only by her bossy sister but, if the overcrowded rooms were any indication, a fair proportion of Cissie's furniture from the staff cottage.

Cosham checked her watch and got up from the table, a plain indication that as far as she was concerned the matter had been dealt with. She wore neat corduroys and a shirt blouse which suited her spare frame and lent an air of gentility to her upright bearing. The woman had been working for the nobs for years and it had rubbed off. Cissie Cosham had accepted a heavy responsibility, first as Zita's children's nanny and later as housekeeper, this record of employment deserving a long-service medal. Mo wondered if the woman had inside information about the Brighams' impending divorce, hence her assurance that all would soon be as before. Mo suspected that secrets were hard to keep in such an upstairs-downstairs situation and, fanned by village gossip, no wonder she was confidently biding her time.

'If that is all, Sergeant, perhaps I can be off. My team will be waiting for me at the Grange to start work.'

Mo stood up, her head almost touching the low beams. 'Not so fast, Mrs Cosham. We have a murder enquiry on

our hands and your evidence may be crucial. May I suggest
we continue this discussion at your cottage? You can, if
you wish, start your cleaners off first but I must insist you
give us your full attention for as long as the police investigation requires it. We could, if you prefer, continue this
interview at Horsham police station.'

The colour drained from Cosham's thin cheeks. 'No need
to get on your high horse with me, miss. Let's get this over
with as quick as possible, shall we? All right if I take my
bike?'

Mo grinned. 'No problem. It's a lovely morning.'

They cycled off together, drawing eyes from every passer-
by. Cosham stared grimly ahead, ignoring the curious
glances of mothers taking their kids to school and the postmistress who watched, open-mouthed, this unlikely
twosome riding past her shop.

They left the bikes at the kitchen entrance and Mo waited
while Mrs Cosham gave her work party their orders. The
single-storey cottage stood on the far side of the paddock
and presented a charming picture, the red-brick porch
supporting a shower of late-blooming yellow roses. Cosham
opened the door and admitted Mo with ill grace, her features
set, irritably reluctant to allow this uninvited visitor into
her home.

Mo diligently wiped her feet and followed her directly
into the dank living room where velvet curtains shut out
all but the sunlight streaming through the front door. Cosham
switched on the light, revealing an interior sparsely furnished
with just a sofa bed, one easy chair, an electric fire and a
low table on which a digital radio had pride of place. An
open door revealed a bare room containing nothing but a
chest of drawers.

'It's very nice here,' Mo remarked. 'You must miss having
a place of your own.'

Cosham moved to the window and flung back the heavy
drapes. 'Just see this garden! I've dug and watered it for
the best part of my life and now look at it – ruined!'

Mo obediently glanced out. Nettles and brambles filled
the borders and the small patch of grass was humped with

molehills. Beyond a wire fence a compost enclosure and a metal brazier stood either side of a back gate leading on to the paddock, the scene enlivened by a rider putting a gleaming black stallion over the jumps.

Mo turned. 'Isn't that Eva's horse, Denzil?'

Cosham drew alongside, her mood softening. 'Yes, and that's my girl in the saddle.' Suddenly, she pulled back and closed the curtains, pulling Mo into the kitchen where a kettle and a single cup and saucer gave her a poignant sense of Cissie Cosham's lonely retreat. Mo pulled out a kitchen chair and suggested they sat down.

'First question, Mrs Cosham. Were you cycling past the Grange late on Wednesday evening? Before you answer, I have to warn you I have firm information about your secret visits here to the cottage.'

'Wickham?'

'Just answer my question, please.' Mo sat, pen poised over her notebook.

Cosham's hand flew to her cheek. 'Well, now you mention it, I did pop over.'

'At what time?'

'Oh, late, very late. I'd better explain about the sleeping arrangements at Bluebell Cottage. It's very old, you see, a farm labourer's place originally. It belonged to our parents, who left it to May because she had looked after them in their old age. Never married, see . . . never had the chance really though May was always the pretty one. Anyway, I was working and this staff cottage suited me so we were both happy. But, as I was saying, May's place is old fashioned and upstairs there are only two bedrooms, one leading off from the other, no landing or anything, so,' she paused, giving a rueful smile, 'you have to pass through my bedroom to reach May's. Poor May suffers from bad nights and has to go down to the loo two or three times a night and, what with her snoring, I'm lucky to get two hours' sleep without her waking me. It causes ructions – not her fault, poor dear, but you can see how losing this place was such a bitter blow. I took to coming here on nights when I couldn't sleep and listening to my little radio.'

'And on Wednesday night?'

'Well, yes, it must have been Wednesday now I come to think about it,' she slyly admitted. 'I went to bed as normal but May had taken one of her pills and I couldn't settle. So I got dressed and came here for a bit of peace. Later, I must have dropped off in the chair.'

'And the time was?'

'I got here about half-past ten or so in time to hear the end of my favourite music programme, *Songs at Sunset* – do you know it? Radio Three.'

'No. But please be sure about this, Mrs Cosham. You cycled past the front of the Grange and saw no visitors' cars?'

'The lights were blazing all over the house like a damn cruise ship. I hate to think what the electricity bills are, I do really. The drive was empty – no callers, I can swear to it.'

'It was raining?'

'Cats and dogs.'

'And what time did you leave?'

'I must have been there two hours – perhaps less, maybe longer.'

'Midnight? One in the morning?'

'Can't say for sure. Like I told you, I dropped off in the chair.'

'And you didn't see anyone either when you arrived or when you left? No cars leaving the estate? Nothing unusual?'

Cosham closed her eyes in patient resignation. 'I've already told you. No one. Nothing. Will that be all?'

Mo closed her notebook. 'For the time being yes, but I may have to speak to you again. If you remember anything later, even something you think unimportant, please contact me immediately. I shall be working from the estate office, as you know.'

Cosham tightened the belt of her raincoat as they left and took a lingering look at her overgrown garden. In the paddock the sunshine gleamed on the glossy coat of the leaping horse, its rider clamped to its back like an incubus.

Mo watched with fascination as horse and rider rose in

the air as if on wings. Suddenly there was a terrible sound of crashing timbers as the rails splintered and the horse plunged out of sight, its rider flying through the air to land in a heap amid the broken poles. Cosham gripped Mo's arm and let out a fearful cry. She flung her off and raced through the garden gate and across the paddock.

The rider was on her knees cradling the horse's head, its mouth foaming, its bloodshot eyes rolling in terror.

Mo knelt beside her. 'Eva! It's you. I'll phone for help, wait here.'

Cosham came lumbering up, tears streaming down her face. Eva looked up, the agony of her instinctive assessment of the horse's injuries all too clear. She cleared her throat and spoke with a decisiveness which took Mo's breath away. 'You get Wickham here damn quick, Coshy. I'll go inside and phone the vet.'

Mo stared at the heaving flank of the suffering animal and gave Cosham a shove. 'I'll wait here, you go and get help.' Already Eva was streaking away towards the big house, Cosham clumsily bringing up the rear.

Eva returned in minutes, Wickham at her heels, Cosham nowhere to be seen. Mo stood aside as Wickham examined the stricken horse. He got to his feet and shook his head. Eva stepped forward and pulled a bolt gun from under her riding mac and, before Mo could utter a cry, shot Denzil through the head.

The horse shuddered, then lay still, blood gushing from the wound and staining the thin turf. Eva dropped the gun and Wickham pulled her into his arms, her sobs rising in the still air like the screams of the damned.

Twenty-Nine

The shooting of the horse threw the investigation into reverse. Brigham arrived back at the Grange but cancelled his appointment with Hayes without explanation and, according to Wickham, was now embedded in a family conference at Zita's house.

Hayes almost felt sorry for the sad beggar: his daughter's fiancé under suspicion of murdering his wife, his ex hysterical at the collapse of the wedding plans and a valuable horse shot dead in his paddock. Whew.

By the time he returned from his talk with the pathologist and was greeted by Mo's news of the dramatic events at the Grange, Clarke was already consulting the police lawyer about the legality of Eva's action and the ownership of the gun. Hayes cornered Sergeant Hedgecoe in the estate office and insisted on an update.

'The gun's an old bolt gun owned by Sir William.'

'Locked up in the gun room?'

'Yes, but Mr Wickham admits that the key to the cabinet was kept on a hook in a cupboard in the boot room next to it.'

Hayes blew his top: the sheer carelessness of it beggared belief. It would have taken Eva only minutes to unlock the gun cabinet, load, and race back to the paddock. He broke into a searing indictment of 'the sheer stupidity of these people' which did no good at all, Hedgecoe withstanding the tirade with a blank response almost bordering on insubordination.

Hayes stormed out, followed by Mo, to join the small party on the paddock loading the horse carcase onto a flatbed truck.

'I think she did the right thing, sir,' Mo put in. 'You weren't there. It was the only decent thing for Eva to do in the circumstances.'

'Sod that! It's complicated the entire investigation. Brigham's off at a tangent dealing with his piddling family ructions while we're stalled on a major murder investigation. Where's the logic in that?'

Mo felt her stomach lurch as they stood beside the vet and watched the gruesome spectacle. Hayes introduced himself and pushed Mo forward. 'My sergeant here was a witness to the accident. You may wish to have a statement from her.'

The vet, a young chap with a harassed expression, regarded Hayes with ill-concealed impatience.

'Thank you, Superintendent, but Mr Wickham has put me in the picture. A tragic accident. Miss Brigham is naturally devastated. Denzil was a special horse, a champion eventer and a huge loss to Sir William in stud fees alone.'

'And the bolt gun? Surely these things are restricted to veterinary use?'

The vet returned Hayes' cold stare with an irritable nod. 'Usually, yes. In fact, I must admit I've never known a private individual having access to such a dangerous firearm. But since 1997 anyone has been able to own a bolt gun to kill animals without a licence, although they can be prosecuted if an animal is destroyed inhumanely. There are persistent rumours that racing greyhounds are sometimes killed in this way. It's cheaper than employing a qualified veterinary surgeon using lethal injections.'

'Then this licence procedure needs tightening up damned quick.'

'Perhaps. On the whole I agree – well, I would, wouldn't I? But it's not top of any governmental agenda and the number of people owning bolt guns must be very few.'

'Why would Sir William need to have one?'

He shrugged. 'That's something you'll have to ask him yourself, Superintendent.'

They talked for a little longer while the removal of the horse was completed and the truck driven off.

Hayes gradually calmed down. As they left the paddock he walked to his car and said, 'We're not going to get anything done here, Prentice. But I shall have to speak to Sir William about this bloody bolt gun later. Let's go back to the pub and get a ploughman's. You can tell me how you got on with Cosham.'

The Red Lion was crowded with locals, the air buzzing with the latest drama at Aspern Grange. Hayes ordered the drinks and they retreated to the back room. Mo still felt queasy and gingerly sipped her lemonade hoping Hayes would delay questioning her in detail about the shooting. In fact he was more concerned with his visit to the pathologist.

'A decent bloke, Doctor Harris. We're in luck here, Prentice, we could have landed up with an opinionated country medic with absolutely no experience of a tricky murder like we've got here.'

'Did he have anything to add to his report, sir?'

'Not professionally but privately conceded we've got no forensic evidence against MacCann. We shall have to let him go just as soon as Clarke and Superintendent Fox admit defeat. They're currently retrieving the MG, which is being transported from the lock-up.'

'Checking for evidence?'

'MacCann doesn't deny being at the Grange the night Suzie was killed, his fingerprints are all over the shop, but unless Clarke can come up with bloodstained clothing or some forensics from the car, he's flogging a dead horse.'

'Ouch!'

He laughed. 'Oh, sorry. A slip of the tongue.'

'We can't hold him much longer?'

'No. Clarke's got a search warrant for MacCann's premises but he's had days to dispose of any incriminating stuff, if there ever was any.'

'You never seriously suspected MacCann, did you, sir?'

He shrugged. 'Wouldn't go as far as to say that: MacCann was there at the witching hour, so to speak, and if he did have a contract from Brigham to kill his wife, he certainly copped a bundle, enough to set himself up in business. Additionally, if he married the daughter he'd have a handle on Brigham for the rest of his life. Now, dig in, Prentice,' he said, pushing the plate of cheese and pickles across the table, 'you look a bit sickly if I may say so. What you need is a bit of grub.'

Hayes blithely picked out the grisly details of the accident between mouthfuls, and Mo attempted to rationalize her recollection of events.

'Mrs Cosham was terribly shocked, burst into tears when she saw the horse fall and Eva shoot up in the air. It must have been a re-run in her mind of the accident which killed the Kipling girl. Mrs Cosham was very fond of the kid, apparently, blamed Suzie, unreasonably, of course, but seeing the same thing happen to Eva in the same paddock must have been a blow between the eyes for her.'

'Where is she now?'

'Back at work.'

'No harm done, then. Tell me about the cottage. You say she couldn't vouch for MacCann leaving before eleven that night?'

Mo quoted from her notes and Hayes looked pensive. 'MacCann's out of luck, then. His mate who owns the lock-up where he garages the MG can't say when the car was returned, which only leaves Clarke with the hope that if he can come up with some forensics to back up a prosecution, the charge will stick.'

His mobile rang and he fumbled in his pocket.

Mo dutifully picked at her lunch, the bile rising with every morsel. She wondered if she was really cut out for this blood-and-guts type of policing. Perhaps, after all, she should have stayed with the Serious Fraud Office.

Hayes shut off his phone and stood. 'Did I say things couldn't get worse, Prentice? Well, I was wrong. Eva Brigham's taken an overdose and has just been admitted to hospital. She's in a coma.'

Thirty

After their scratch lunch Hayes told Mo to accompany him to Zita's house and try to flush out Brigham.

'Surely he will be at Eva's bedside?'

'Doubt it. With the mess he's in I reckon he'll leave that to Zita. We need to talk to him now, Prentice, while he's on the back foot, while he's unsure what song MacCann is singing in the interview room.'

'But Macey, the lawyer, will give him a full report, won't he?'

'Macey's almost as much in the dark as Clarke while they're still pulling the MG to pieces.'

'Perhaps we could move in on the shop while they're searching?'

'A long shot, more useful as a frightener for MacCann if you ask me. Still, we might as well take a gander while Clarke's merry men are taking the MG apart. It's on our way.'

The shop was cordoned off and already attracting curious onlookers. 'Bad for business,' Hayes remarked, 'even if the poor guy's innocent.'

MacCann's assistant, a girl who answered to Mary Ross under Hayes' questioning, stood in the midst of chaos. MacCann's precious items for sale had been turned out from cabinets and cupboards, the storeroom stripped, every possible cranny unnecessarily pillaged, in Hayes' view. 'What do they think they're looking for, for God's sake?'

'Bloodstained clothing?'

'Well, it's not likely to be lurking under a Minton teapot, is it? Let's go upstairs.'

MacCann's flat was in the process of being taken apart by two uniformed coppers whose refusal to allow Hayes and Mo to poke about was hardly unexpected. The accommodation comprised two intercommunicating rooms plus a kitchen and bathroom, the third floor offering an attic bedroom overlooking the square.

After a cursory glance and a polite exchange with the officers, Hayes went back downstairs where Mo was chatting with Mary Ross. He threw her a sharp look and hurried back to the car.

'Bloody waste of time,' he said dismissively, revving up the engine with a heavy foot on the accelerator. Mo settled in the passenger seat idly regarding the passing scene. The horse-chestnut trees were already shedding their leaves, the recent rainstorm lashing down scores of shiny conkers which lay in the gutters like a miser's hoard.

'There was one thing, sir. You said no one knew about the MG but Suzie.'

'And the shop assistant.'

'Yes, well, Mary said Eva knew about it too. She'd spotted Freddie driving back from a house auction one night and pulled his leg about it. Offered to buy him a new sports car as a wedding present.'

'Nice one.'

'Well, if Eva saw it who knows who else had seen MacCann cruising round in his old banger? Mrs Cosham, for instance. If she *had* spied the MG tucked away in the copse that night she would have immediately sussed that Freddie was cheating on her best girl.'

'Best girl? What the hell do you mean by that?'

'Listen. If she brought up the Brigham kids before they were shunted off to boarding school, I bet Eva was her favourite. Just like Cosham took a shine to the Kipling child, the one who died.'

'You think Cosham told Eva of her suspicions?'

'She didn't have the chance, did she? Suzie was killed before Cosham could warn Eva, and I can't see her deliberately breaking the girl's heart about Freddie's larks after that. Eva's still in love with the guy, plans to marry him in a few weeks. You saw her at Zita's tea party – she wasn't cancelling the wedding, was she?'

They drew up outside Zita's house, where an impressive Bentley took pride of place at the kerb.

'Looks as though Brigham's back on the nest already,' Hayes dourly remarked as they approached the front door. The maid let them in, her nervous greeting breaking into a smile that lit up the fast-fading dusk. 'Madam's expecting you,' she said brightly and led them through to the drawing room, where the grieving parents sat side by side on the brocade sofa. Any suggestion that Zita would be by her daughter's hospital cot was clearly well wide of the mark. Her blotched features owed as much to an emergency raid on the gin bottle as motherly tears.

'It's the doctor, madam,' the maid announced.

'Oh, for Christ's sake get back to the kitchen, Elsie!' Brigham shouted. She scurried out, leaving the door ajar. 'Stupid bloody girl. She's hopeless, Zita. Where on earth did you get her?'

'The agency,' Zita murmured, burying her face in a handkerchief.

Brigham ominously got to his feet, forcing Hayes and Mo to draw back. 'Listen, Superintendent, this is a private matter. I suggest you postpone your enquiries until a more appropriate time. My daughter is at death's door thanks to you lot. Harassing her fiancé, making criminal accusations, no wonder my poor girl took an overdose.'

'The shooting of her horse didn't help,' Hayes put in with surprising restraint. 'Perhaps we could have a few words in private, sir, just to clear up the financial arrangements you agreed with our suspect.'

Brigham exploded with a barrage of invective, setting Zita off in a fresh paroxysm of weeping. Mo stood her ground, wondering if Hayes was really so insensitive or this was just the way he normally took advantage of stressful situations. And, not to put too fine a point on it, nothing could match the stress Sir William must be feeling, poised between his inebriated ex-wife and a daughter's attempted suicide – if that was what it was.

After more polite argy-bargy, Sir William agreed to accompany them into the next room and they sat down together at Zita's Louis something reproduction dining table.

'My lawyer should be in on this,' Brigham tersely remarked, seating himself with ill grace, 'but let's just get on with it, shall we? There's bugger all to add to what I said at our previous meeting at Lincoln's Inn.'

And, as it turned out, despite Hayes' persistent interrogation, Sir William stood firm. The money transaction had been a wedding gift, and his late wife's pregnancy had been a delightful surprise. 'A gift from the gods,' he smoothly intoned, exhaustively refuting any divorce proceedings in the offing, and curtly reminding Hayes that 'At sixty-three years of age, sir, I am perfectly able to sire more children, as my physician, Doctor Hammond, will, at my request, readily affirm.'

And stick that in your pipe and smoke it, Mo said to herself. What a put-down! They were smartly ejected onto the pavement by Sir William himself with no sloppy attendance from the hapless Elsie.

'One more thing, Sir William. The bolt gun. Why would you keep something as dangerous as that in your house?'

'Oh, that old thing! Surprised it still works,' he snapped. 'It's not illegal, Hayes. Frankly, I'd forgotten all about it. It belonged to my father, since you ask. In his twenties he was doing his National Service at Aldershot, waiting to be transferred to officer training at Sandhurst. He was detailed to work in the army abattoir, poor sod, just sweeping up, menial jobs, nothing to do with killing the poor beasts. Got the old man in the gut, turned vegetarian for months after that, wouldn't touch a rare steak for a ransom. Anyway, he made off with this bolt gun and it's been in the family ever since. Sort of souvenir.'

'Really? You must be very interested in macabre souvenirs, Sir William, keeping that shillelagh in the hall to amuse your house guests and a bolt gun in the gun room. Funny sense of humour, if I may say so.'

'Just remember your place, young man. You are exceeding your brief, Hayes – I shall have to recommend your diligence to Commander Crick,' he sourly added.

But before Hayes allowed Brigham to shut the door in his face he posed one last shot. 'As a matter of interest, Sir William, who is at your daughter's bedside at this critical juncture?'

'Not that it's any business of yours, Superintendent, but we do have loyal staff to call upon. Mrs Cosham is in attendance.'

Thirty-One

There didn't seem much they could do after that except drive over to Horsham to see how the examination of MacCann's MG was progressing.

Clarke drew them both outside the police workshop and lit a cigarette.

'How's it going, Inspector?'

He looked grim. 'Nothing so far but it's a nitpicking operation and may take hours yet. The forensic team are supervising my mechanics. Any joy at your end?'

Hayes described the lack of findings at the antique shop followed by an abrasive encounter with Sir William. He brightened. 'But don't look so miserable, Clarke, we're due for a breakthrough. Just one piece of evidence pinning MacCann to the murder will do the trick. Is his lawyer playing up?'

'Macey? The usual tantrums but we've got till tomorrow to arrest him or let the blighter go.'

Mo loitered at the fringe of this exchange, wondering what miracle DI Clarke hoped to pull out of the hat.

After a further check on the progress of the car search, Hayes and his attractive sidekick strolled back to their car. Clarke morosely pondered if there was a special dispensation for these so-called special agents: with promotion, for instance, they qualified not only for carpeted offices but better-looking sergeants. Hedgecoe was no comparison. No way.

Next morning the foul weather returned with a vengeance, reducing the Red Lion's beer garden to a muddy grotto. Hayes stared out at the rain and decided to give the countryside a miss for the day and push off back to the smoke. 'If you drop me off at the station for the early train, Prentice, I can make it back here by two by which time Clarke will have released his suspect.'

'You're not expecting anything from the MG, then, sir?'

'Difficult to say but I want to talk to Bennet about Sir William's stance in all this. I'm still not satisfied.'

'You want me to stay here?'

'You keep an eye on the sharp end, girl. Ring me if there's any news. You'll need the car.'

This last admission cheered her. The business of having no transport was a sore point.

After driving away from the station Mo headed back to the village to follow up a little enquiry of her own. May Cripps knew more about this case than she dared to admit but while her sister was detailed to hospital watch, the chance of getting her alone was too good to miss.

The windscreen wipers swished rhythmically as she made her way down the High Street. A knot of hopefuls queued at the bus stop, chewing over the trouble at the big house, Mo guessed. The car screeched to a stop and skidded in the wet as she drew alongside the bus shelter. Winding down the window, Mo shouted to a stout figure in a plastic mac standing at the kerb.

'Hey, Miss Cripps, is that you? Can I give you a lift?'

The four other prospective passengers looked up expectantly then pushed May forward. She hurried to the car, beaming.

'Get in, you'll get soaked waiting about. Are you going into town?'

'The supermarket. It's my weekly shop. You sure it's not out of your way, dear?'

'No, of course not. Put your shopper in the back.'

May Cripps settled in the passenger seat and gave a contented sigh. They set off at a good lick and were soon parked in the supermarket forecourt.

'Actually, I was hoping to have a word with you, Miss Cripps. Have you time for a coffee? The cafe here is handy.'

'That's very nice of you. Sergeant Prentice, isn't it? Nasty job you had seeing that poor horse shot down dead in front of you. Cissie was just beside herself.'

They walked through to the coffee shop and found a quiet corner table. May shook out her mac and folded it away inside her shopping bag before settling down with a mug of tea and a muffin. She wore a lacy knitted cardigan which must have filled many evening hours in front of the television. The two sisters were hardly alike and it was apparent that May had retained a prettiness despite the years, her eyes blue as forget-me-nots.

'You wanted to ask me about poor Eva, I expect,' she said, cutting her muffin into bite-size pieces.

'Er, yes, of course. How is she? I heard that your sister is by her bedside waiting for good news.'

'Poor Cissie dotes on that girl, you know. Brought her up when her mother was on the stage.'

'Away from home a good deal, I suppose.'

'Lovely voice she had. Made loads of records and sang in all the top opera houses, you know. Famous, she was.'

'Cissie must have missed the children when they went away to school.'

'Loves kiddies, my sister does. Such a sad thing, neither of us lucky in the family way. And then she took a shine to the little Kipling girl, said she reminded her of me when I was little. Fancy that!' May flushed, her cheek rosy under a dusting of face powder.

'I hope you don't mind me asking you, Miss Cripps, but you remember the night poor Lady Brigham died? Mrs Cosham mentioned to me that she couldn't sleep and cycled off back to her cottage. That's right, isn't it? Don't be anxious, Miss Cripps, her secret visits to her old home at night are known about, Wickham noticed her going there after dark and mentioned it to Lady Brigham, who understood how she felt, and let it be. But you did hear her go out that night after you went to bed, didn't you?'

'Well, no, I didn't. I'd taken a sleeping pill you see and it really knocks me out. But later I woke up in such a fright.'

'You heard her come back?'

'Cissie is very considerate, tries ever so hard not to disturb me, but that night I woke up in a terrible sweat. It was this vixen in the woods, calling to her mate I suppose but have you ever heard them cry, miss? Terrible screams, just like a young girl being attacked. Turned my blood cold. Then I realized what it really was and tried to get back to sleep. But I kept tossing and turning like you do and I dare not take another pill. After a bit I heard Cissie's key in the lock and her settling down. It was late, I guessed that, because I was wide awake, my pill had worn off and once you're disturbed like that it's the very devil to get off again, don't you find?'

Mo pressed her. 'Did you look at the clock?'

May frowned. 'Mm. Really worried, I was. Cissie had been out for hours. Half past six! I couldn't believe it.'

'Did you mention it to her next morning?'

May drew back. 'Oh, no. Cissie hates to think she's being spied on. Likes her privacy she does and who can blame her, having to share with me after years of independence?'

Mo politely let the conversation run on smoother lines and when May had finished her tea they parted. 'Oh, look, the rain's stopped,' May exclaimed with pleasure.

Mo drove back to the Grange and checked with Hedgecoe about the current state of play.

'Oh, MacCann's out. We had to let him go.'

'Nothing in the car? Not even a screw of cocaine to hold him on?'

Hedgecoe shook his head. 'And your boss? What's the Superintendent up to this morning?'

'Gone back to London to talk to the man in charge.'

He gave a wry grin. 'Thought sending a top detective from Scotland Yard would roll up this murder in double-quick time, eh? They can't write us off on this one, your lot's done no better than us when it comes to catching villains, eh?'

Mo made a rapid retreat and sat in the car mulling over May Cripps' account of her sister's night out. Why would Cissie lie? The discrepancy was too wide to ignore and Mo's gut feeling went with May's version.

She slowly drew away and parked on the far side of the
paddock, the field now deserted, Cissie's cottage a dark
silhouette against the cloudy sky.

On impulse she strode over to the boundary and vaulted
the cottage fence. The doors and windows were all secured,
the thick curtains shutting out any prying eyes. Mo wandered
round the overgrown garden where rabbits had nibbled away
at the bedraggled dahlias still bravely sporting a few shaggy
blooms, the last hurrah of the season.

She turned back to the paddock and was passing the
compost heap when a shred of black plastic caught her eye,
the rotting vegetation scuffed aside by, at a guess, rats. She
poked about in the odorous mess with a bamboo cane and
eventually got a grip on a rubbish bag.

Pulling it out, she undid the knot with gloved hands. The
contents were stiff but dry and after gingerly unrolling the
bundle a cursory examination made it all too clear. Mo
drew a sharp breath and anxiously scanned the paddock.
Still empty. She called Hayes.

'That breakthrough you were hoping for, sir. I think we've
got it. I've found a bag of bloodstained clothing hidden just
beyond the paddock.' She quickly filled in details of the
location, and after a further hasty exchange he told her to
be at the station to meet him at midday.

'What shall I do with it, sir?'

'Pack it up again and put it back where it was. We'll just
have to hope it stays hidden till I get there with Clarke.
What have you got? Trousers? A shirt?'

'A mac, sir. A woman's hooded raincoat and bloodstained
woollen gloves.'

Thirty-Two

Mo dared not hang about the paddock to fill in time, drawing attention to her discovery would almost be worse than losing it. She glanced at her watch and wondered how she could be seen to be acting naturally for the hour until Hayes was to be picked up from the station.

Mulling over her conversation with May Cripps that morning, it was becoming increasingly clear that the poor woman would be called upon to speak up against her sister's version of her night out, a situation to tax the most self-assured witness. Chances were she would back off, pretend to have been confused when Hayes tried to confirm it. Poor May. Caught between a rock and a hard place.

She left the car outside the estate office and walked to Wickham's cottage where, if fortune was really on her side, Tracey would be at home.

But she was out of luck. Bill Wickham opened the door, his work clothes spattered with muck.

'Yes?' he barked, not the warmest of greetings but Mo ploughed on, making it up as she went along, hoping her activity around the village would be regarded by all those invisible watching eyes as part of the police routine.

'May I come in?'

'I was just getting changed. Been clearing out Denzil's stable. Is it important?'

He reluctantly allowed her inside and tossed his wet pullover into the sink.

'Coffee?' he asked, putting on, Mo had to admit, a deter-mined show of compliance.

'No, thanks, I won't keep you. Just a few questions.'

'I give my opinion to the vet. He's quite satisfied. You've

been around horses, miss, I guessed that when we went off
for that gallop over the downs. You've got to agree Eva
took the only humane course. Poor kid's taken it bad. In a
coma, I heard. Any news?'

'Not so far. She could come round at any time.'

'Or not at all,' he brusquely countered.

'On another point, Mr Wickham, I gather you were aware
of Mrs Cosham's return visits to her cottage and reported
it to Lady Brigham. Did she take any action as far as you
know? Confront her about it? Repeat the allegations to Sir
William?'

'No, Suzie wasn't the vindictive type. She had a bad time
from the old bag right from the start but I would have heard
if there had been a showdown.'

'You didn't see Mrs Cosham out late on Wednesday
night? After you got back from the pub, say?'

He shook his head. 'I've already told the DI all I know.
Saw no one, not MacCann nor his motor.'

'But you checked on the stables before you turned in?'

'As always.'

Mo stifled a sigh. 'Look, now that Lady Brigham is dead
you don't have to be discreet, any private information you
have could be vital. Did you know about a possible relationship with Frederick MacCann?'

'No, I didn't and even if I had suspicions I wouldn't be
gabbing to Sir William about it neither.'

Further veiled hints got Mo nowhere, Wickham remaining
the very picture of the loyal retainer. That was the trouble
with these people, blast it. Too much obeisance and a determination to cling on to the traditional way of seeing and
hearing no evil.

Mo threw a bouncer. 'Why did you decline to offer a
DNA sample, Mr Wickham?'

His face darkened. 'Why the bloody hell should I?'

At that inconvenient moment the door swung open and
Tracey bounced into the kitchen. Mo hastily got to her feet,
and shoved her notebook in her pocket. 'Hi, Tracey. You
been dragged in on Mrs Cosham's spring clean?'

Mo escaped, leaving Wickham to talk himself out of it,

and drove to the station. There was still ten minutes before Hayes' train was due and so she wandered into Gilbert's Taxi Hire office, where an elderly cove was checking the sports results on Teletext. He looked up. 'Can I help you, miss?'

Mo produced her warrant card, which made him sit up. 'Just a routine enquiry, sir. You have heard about the murder investigation going on in Flodde? One small question. You keep an account for the Brighams, I understand. Is that right?'

He nodded. 'I've run a tab for the family for years but mostly for milady since the young 'uns got their own transport.'

'Lady Zita Brigham, you mean?'

'Yes, of course. The other Lady Brigham always drove herself. Never used the train, not as far as I know anyhow.'

'But Eva Brigham, the daughter, was a regular pick-up at weekends?'

'On and off. Mostly Friday nights but sometimes she got a lift down with her brother. Nice young lady, had this library job at some college in London, didn't have to work Saturdays, see, which let her keep an eye on her mum, who hasn't been so well lately.' He lowered his head, reluctant to elaborate, but Mo thought, Odds on this taxi bloke knows all about Zita being banned for drink driving. It was just the sort of stuff to hit the headlines in the local rag and the old man was never going to jeopardize good relations with his best customer now that her requirements must have trebled.

'You can see the passengers leaving the station from your office here?'

'Have to keep an eye out, don't I? To pick up me regulars.'

'And how late do you work, Mr Gilbert?'

'Depends. But now I'm near retirement I usually chuck it in about eight once the rush hour thins out.'

'Unless you have a late booking like your regular pick-up for Miss Brigham on Friday nights?'

'That's about it.'

'Then you don't miss much, do you, Mr Gilbert?'

'Not a lot,' he conceded.

'Did you run Miss Brigham home on Wednesday night?'

His eyes flickered towards the computer screen. 'Definitely not, miss. That was the final of the snooker on the telly. Wouldn't miss that – you ask my wife!' he added with a chuckle.

Mo quickly turned, jerked to attention by the arrival of the midday train.

'Thanks, Mr Gilbert. You've been very helpful,' she said over her shoulder on the way out.

Hayes was in great form, more excited than she had ever seen him.

'Quick, drive straight back to the paddock, Prentice, Clarke should be there by now.'

The recovery of the plastic bin liner from the compost was a huge relief to Mo, who had visions of a posse of policemen assembling in Cosham's backyard only to find the evidence whisked away.

Clarke took charge of the sodden bundle and they followed his car back to the forensics lab. Mo cooled her heels in the outer office, anxiously pacing out the cramped waiting room while Clarke's pathologist made an emergency examination of the raincoat and gloves.

Hayes emerged triumphant, punching the air and grabbing Mo in a very unprofessional bear hug. 'Eureka! Suzie's blood, no question, and our vengeful servant, Cissie Cosham, in the target area.'

'The mac's hers?'

'We'll see, but she's certainly got some explaining to do. Clarke's already sent Hedgecoe to the hospital to bring her in.'

Mo felt her fingers tingle, a reaction all too familiar from her former painstaking analyses of fraudsters' balance sheets. Yes! A hit. A palpable hit.

Thirty-Three

Mo drove Hayes to the station, where Cissie Cosham was already installed in the interview room. It was agreed that DI Clarke and Hayes would conduct the interrogation and, having confirmed that their suspect refused to have a legal representative, they wasted no time in getting down to business.

After the formal preliminaries Clarke punched off with a straight left.

'Now, I have here in this evidence bag a coat and gloves recovered from your cottage garden. Do you recognize these garments, Mrs Cosham?'

She sat bolt upright in the chair, her face pale as death, dark circles round her eyes evidence of her night vigil at Eva's bedside.

She nodded.

'Please speak up for the recording, Mrs Cosham.'

She coughed. 'Yes, they're mine.'

'Did you place them in a refuse bag and hide these items under the compost?'

'Yes, I did.'

'Must I remind you that anything you say—'

'I know all that!' she spat out, her eyes flashing. 'You don't have to repeat everything, I'm not stupid.'

Hayes butted in. 'No, of course not, but you are suspected of a very serious crime, Mrs Cosham, and I recommend that you have a solicitor present. We can postpone this interview if you wish and obtain the services of a lawyer for you if necessary.'

She stiffened, her steely resolve almost saintly. 'No need. I prefer to get this over with. The mac is mine and also the gloves. I hid them while my mind was confused after the murder. I make no excuses. I killed Lady Brigham. She deserved it. The woman was evil and when this is all over everything will be back to normal.'

This extraordinary confession took Hayes totally by surprise. Without so much as a nudge this stoical creature had laid her head on the block. 'I must insist you have professional advice,' he said, ignoring Clarke's dismay.

'All right,' she said indifferently. 'But I shan't change my mind. Only I need to warn my sister. Can I phone her?'

'Yes, of course.'

She was escorted back to a cell while Clarke organized a continuation of the interview at four in the afternoon. Hayes waited for him in his office, Prentice tagging along, her astonishment at the acceleration of events as great as his.

'Do you think she's unbalanced?' she asked. 'Shouldn't we get a psychologist's report, sir? The poor woman's been without sleep at Eva's bedside since she was brought into hospital.'

Hayes brushed this aside, critically examining the file in front of him and making notes in the margins.

Mo was chancing her arm interrupting him yet again but felt impelled to get her point across. After all, she was the one who had found the damned bundle in Cissie's garden. 'One small thing, sir?' she ventured. 'When I found the bag I had a quick look inside and it struck me that the mac was a pricey item for a middle-aged domestic to spend her money on.'

He looked up irritably. 'Well?'

'Aquascutum, sir. A designer label my mother favoured. A shop for ladies, she always said. It has a flagship store on Regent Street.'

'So what? These people get hand-me-downs from their employers. Zita could have given it to her years ago.'

'Not her size.'

'A charity shop, then. All sorts of flash gear gets recycled at Oxfam, so I hear. You're nit-picking, Prentice, a woman like Cosham would seize on a bargain like that. Forget it.'

Mo let it go, and, on reflection, she had been impressed

with Cosham's style, which was a far cry from May's cosy outfits.

The interview resumed later that afternoon with a Mr Smythson at Cosham's side, a nervous young man who was fearful that the briefing with his reluctant client was seriously lacking.

Clarke pressed ahead, restarting the recording equipment and putting his suspect through the necessary preliminaries approved by her legal adviser.

'Shall we hear your version of Wednesday evening's events? In your own time, Mrs Cosham. We just need to get at the truth,' Hayes stressed, giving Clarke a firm indication that acquiring a watertight confession was dependent on the unwritten rules of engagement, especially when dealing with a suspect like Cissie Cosham.

Her manner was extraordinarily contained, hardly the demeanour of a person who had never been in police custody before.

She set off at a smart pace. 'My hatred of Suzie had been boiling up for years and if I had been a younger woman I would have given in my notice as soon as she appeared on the scene. My Lady Brigham would have taken me on but the cottage was my only home and it went with the job at the Grange.'

'But she turned you out,' Clarke couldn't resist pointing out.

'Yes, and I did seriously think of leaving then but Lady Brigham couldn't offer me anything but an attic room at the top of her house and I hoped, at the back of my mind, Sir William would reverse his new wife's decision. I soldiered on, living at my sister's and waiting for the marriage to break up, which it was on the verge of doing after that poor little Kipling girl got killed owing to the criminal carelessness of that gold-digger. She got the message then: the village folk turned against her and the county set would not accept an upstart like an ex-model, for heaven's sake, especially as Sir William was living abroad for most of the time.'

'But you hoped to get your house back if there was a divorce?'

'Yes, I did. Then I found out about the baby.'

'You knew Lady Brigham was pregnant?'

She smiled sourly, and raised an eyebrow. 'You can't keep stuff like that secret from the staff, Inspector. Tracey found a testing kit in madam's waste bin in her bathroom and brought it to show me. Thrilled to bits she was. That silly girl was dazzled by the new milady and all excited at the prospect of children in the Grange after all this time. I told her to hold her tongue but the symptoms were all too obvious when she started vomiting before breakfast. If Sir William had been at home even he couldn't have missed it.'

'You suspected there was a lover involved?'

She was terribly shocked. 'A man friend, you mean? Of course not! The baby was a Brigham all right and that was the problem. Once Sir William knew about it, any hopes I had of a divorce and Lady Zita being back in charge flew out of the window. He's not the man to desert his wife or throw nasty accusations about.'

'But you found out about Freddie MacCann?'

'Not till after the murder, and I still can't believe it. They were very clever. That vixen was a nasty piece of work but playing fast and loose with the master was just too much!'

Clarke glanced at Hayes in clear disbelief but Hayes motioned her to continue. 'Let's get to the night she died. You left home you said and spent an hour or two at your cottage before cycling back to your sister's.'

She paused, gathering her thoughts as if the night in question had been years away. 'No, that's not right. I lied to you about that. I did go to my cottage like I said. May was having one of her snoring fits and it really got on my nerves. Worked myself up into a proper paddy about it, finding myself forced out in the pouring rain just to get a bit of peace.'

'But you didn't see anyone or any vehicle?'

'No, I'm certain of it. I pushed on to the cottage, made myself a nice cup of tea and settled down with my little radio. It was all so cosy it only made me madder. How could a tart like that turn me out of my home? I simmered about it and eventually decided to have it out with her once and for all.'

'So late?'

'Oh, she kept terrible hours that one, stayed up half the night burning every light in the house like I told you. I knew I'd best say my piece while I was still fired up about it. If Sir William was going to settle down and raise a new family I might as well stake my claim to the cottage before they moved a nursery maid in.'

'So far from the house? Surely not,' Clarke insisted.

'Well, *I* was put there when Lady Zita employed me to look after her children, wasn't I?' A note of defiance was sparking up which Hayes was anxious to defuse. If they were to get a viable confession out of this woman an unconfrontational atmosphere was imperative. The solicitor asked Cosham if she wished to continue but the look she gave him would have shrivelled a lesser man.

Hayes urged her on.

'I got togged up again and set off for the Grange. I had my keys, let myself in and called up to her. She was upstairs playing that trashy music of hers so loud she didn't hear me at first. I shouted again, not wishing to have a set-to with madam in her boudoir so to speak, and after a bit she condescended to come down. Stark naked, would you believe! A deliberate insult to me, of course, she didn't regard staff as being worth her time getting dressed.'

She sipped a glass of water and glanced at the wall clock, suddenly breaking off to enquire if Eva had woken from the coma.

'Not so far, Mrs Cosham, but don't worry, I'm sure someone has taken your place at her bedside.'

'Her young man, I expect,' she said with satisfaction. 'Once all this has blown over they'll be happy again. He wasn't guilty, you know. If you had charged him I would have come forward.'

'You were saying Lady Brigham joined you in the hall.'

She smiled. 'Ah, yes. I suggested she got something warm

on – the house was always damp, you know – and that we
went into the study as there was something we needed to
get settled about my future employment. She wouldn't have
it. Laughed in my face, she did. I put my conditions about
staying on and told her I knew about the baby. That really
got her, and she tried to throw me out. We struggled in the
hall, I grabbed the stick from the umbrella stand and tried
to make her listen, but she broke away and tried to run
upstairs. I chased after her, slipped, and accidentally caught
her foot in my stick and she fell with a tremendous wallop,
blood streaming from a cut on her head. Then, I don't know
what came over me, but seeing all that blood proper fired
me up, and before she could scramble up, I hit her a good
whack, sending her sprawling, losing her footing. Those
silly sandals of hers are more of a hindrance than proper
bedroom slippers.'

The solicitor looked aghast, wondering if this stupid cow
was going to dig herself in even further, and with the scent
of success burning a hole in his patience, Hayes threw a
clincher.

'Then you hit her again and again, Mrs Cosham?'

'That's right. Well, after the first one I just piled in, couldn't
stop I couldn't. But when I came to my senses I knew it was
time to make my way home. But my mac was all bloody
and my nice woollen gloves stained. Nothing for it but to
get back to the cottage as soon as I could, change into another
coat and bury everything under the compost till the heat died
down and I had a chance to burn it.'

'You keep spare clothing at the cottage?'

'Oh, yes, all my winter clothes are stored there. Poor May
hasn't room in her wardrobe for my things as well as her
own, and I've always been a fancy dresser, my only luxury
you could say.'

Thirty-Four

Three weeks later Eva Brigham awoke from her coma. Sleeping Beauty's eyes flickered just for a moment, but there was no Prince Charming to break the spell with a kiss; only her brother, Renton.

He had been doing his stint of bedside watch, talking inconsequently, occasionally humming a few bars of her favourite songs, finally reading aloud from the sports pages if inspiration failed. And at last it had all paid off. He leapt to his feet and shouted for a nurse. 'Eva's awake! Quick, quick! Bring someone, for God's sake, before she slips away again.'

Her recovery after that was rapid, and shortly before Christmas she was discharged from the private clinic and allowed home under supervision. The blank weeks she had missed were carefully filtered, her psychiatrist anxious not to precipitate another breakdown. But gradually the news of Cissie Cosham's arrest broke through and Zita had her work cut out restraining her. Frequent outbursts of tears followed by frenzied tantrums about the non-appearance of Freddie MacCann were hard to handle, and Renny, taking the brunt of his sister's temper, moved back home, Sir William fully occupied in London by legal entanglements involved in selling Aspern Grange.

Mo returned to Flodde to sign off Hayes' involvement in the investigation and tie up the loose ends. Cosham was due to appear in court for the first time to confirm her guilty plea, Sir William refusing to assist in any aspect of her defence. But Zita, loyal to her long-term housekeeper and friend, appointed a top barrister to represent her. Not that the lawyer had much to work with; Cosham remained tight-lipped over the details of that fatal night and without Zita's insistence he would have washed his hands of this wretched client, writing her off as uncooperative in the extreme. To her credit, Cissie Cosham put on a good front, her immaculate appearance only marred by the astonishing transformation of her careful coiffure, her hair now snow white and smoothly drawn back in a velvet band.

Mo decided to drop in at MacCann's antiques gallery on her way back to London, curious as to the way Mary Ross was coping with Freddie's disappearance after his release from custody.

The shop had undergone subtle redecoration, and was now tastefully repainted a mousy beige, which set off the glowing colours of numerous gilt-framed pictures lining the walls. A mahogany table had been dragged to the centre of the room and set out with gleaming silver, a collection of hand bells and a miscellaneous selection of letter openers. Freddie MacCann was more than lucky, his assistant had a real flair and, if the cluster of excited customers just leaving was any indication, the shop was doing good business.

Mo waited for Mary's last buyer to leave before entering, the winter sunlight fading as the afternoon drew to a close. Mary greeted her with instant recognition and enthusiastically showed her round, pointing out her improvements.

'Freddie's given me carte blanche, asked me to stay in charge until after Easter at the earliest. Lets me do the buying and everything. I've even got a part-time helper at weekends.'

'Well, that's fantastic. You deserve a break. Where's he hiding out?'

Mary put a warning finger to her lips and drew Mo into the annexe where her desk and the cash box were tucked away. 'Shush, he's upstairs. Packing. Just off back to Aspen for Christmas.'

'Wow! That's expensive.'

'Didn't you hear? He's about to come into money. Suzie Brigham made a will, left all her personal stuff plus her half share in Sir William's property to Freddie.'

'The Grange?'

Mary nodded, alert for sounds from the flat above. 'And the London mews house,' she whispered. 'There's going to be a court case, Sir William is contesting the will, of course, but he doesn't seem to have a leg to stand on.'

'Blimey!'

'It's astonishing, isn't it? Twelve months ago poor Freddie hadn't a bean to bless himself with and now he's planning to start a ski school in Zermatt. I'm crossing my fingers he'll let me stay on here as manager, I could never afford to buy him out.' She suddenly grabbed Mo's arm, hearing heavy footsteps on the stairs. They both swung round, like guilty schoolgirls caught smoking behind the bike sheds.

Freddie dropped his bulging sports bag and came over, greeting Mo like a long-lost friend, his tanned features breaking into a wide smile. 'Hey, get you! It's Sergeant Prentice, isn't it? Looking great, too. Nice to see you. What brings you down here?'

He looked as fit as an ad for expensive aftershave, his athletic frame now smoothly kitted out in leather trousers and a sports jacket.

'Just popped in to say cheerio to Mary. I'm off the case now, on my way back to chase real villains. Mary's done a wonderful job for you here,' she added, stemming a burning curiosity to ask Freddie about his love life.

'Bloody marvellous girl,' he enthused, then, grabbing his bag, was about to make his getaway when the door burst open and Eva appeared, her eyes wild, looking for all the world like an avenging angel.

'I knew you'd be here, you bastard. Thought you could slip in and be away again before I caught up with you. Still kept the MG though, I see, saw it parked in the back lane. Can't part with it even now you can afford a fucking Ferrari?'

'Don't talk tosh, Eva,' he said evenly, attempting to gently push past.

'Wasn't screwing this shop out of Dad enough for you, Freddie? Had to get stupid Suzie to top up your gigolo fund as well?'

'That was *her* idea! It was a joke, Eva. We never thought

it would ever materialize, of course we didn't. Suzie set it
up for insurance, she said, in case William found out about
us and shot her dead. She wasn't seriously worried, but you
know what Suzie was like, thought everything was good
for a laugh.'

'Yeah, sure!' Eva moved closer, her eyes narrowing. Mo
tried to butt in but she pushed her aside, snatching a stiletto
letter opener from the table and waving it wildly. Freddie
tried to calm her down but the girl was trembling with fury.

'I just got your letter,' she spat, shoving an envelope in
his face. 'Good of you to write, Freddie, nice of you to
give me a final brush-off before you jetted off back to your
skiing pals. You thought you'd escape before I could reach
you. You were always so sure of yourself, Freddie MacCann,
but I'm not letting you get away with it. Coshie did it for
us, for Christ's sake! And all for nothing. She said we would
be together once Suzie was gone but she didn't know you,
did she? First chance you get, you take the money and run.'

Mo took a step forward but stumbled over his bag as
Eva jumped aside and, in one swift movement, had lunged
at Freddie, slashed at his chest, and then, raising the knife,
stabbed him again, the two of them locked in a deadly
scuffle. Mary screamed and grabbed the phone on her
desk while Mo grappled with Eva, Freddie now slumped
against a Chinese cabinet, blood bubbling from his mouth,
his eyes glazing over. Mo managed to subdue Eva, disarm
her and propel the sobbing girl to a chair, fearful of taking
her eyes off her yet horribly aware that Freddie was the
real emergency.

Mary got through to the police and ran into the street
screaming for help. A pair of passing traffic wardens
rushed back with her and in minutes the small shop was
crammed with appalled witnesses. The sound of the ambu-
lance bell was like music to Mo's ears and in its wake a
police car was on the scene and, at Mo's insistence, took
charge of Eva.

She followed the screaming sirens to the hospital accompanied by a constable who later drove her to the station to
make a formal statement.

It was only as she was signing the report that witnessing Cosham's signature on her confession came to mind, the memory of it poised like a breakdown in the smooth running of a newsreel: Cosham was right-handed.

Thirty-Five

W hen the crowd had dispersed and Mary Ross stood alone in the shop, the full impact of events struck her like a hammer blow. What if Freddie died?

She slumped on the chesterfield and surveyed with horror the scattered objects that had been knocked to the floor in the course of the scuffle. Blood pooled on the Persian rug amid the chaos, Freddie's bag kicked under the table and fragments of broken china everywhere.

Tears welled up but, with determined fortitude, she decided to go into the back room and make herself a strong cup of tea. Everyone had rushed off without a word. Was the place to be regarded as some sort of crime scene? Was she supposed to leave it until the police told her what to do? The shop must be closed for the present, no question, but for how long? And if Freddie did die where did she stand from a business point of view?

Mary dried her eyes and looked out at the back lane where Freddie's sports car stood under the street lights where, for security, he always parked it. She washed up the tea things and decided to seek out Mo Prentice. Mo would know what had to be done. With an urgency born of a practical plan of action Mary Ross put on her coat and was about to lock up when she noticed an envelope under the chair. It was addressed to Eva Brigham. She put it in her bag, doused the lights and drove to the police station.

Hayes had set off from London like a rocket as soon as Mo phoned with the news.

'For Christ's sake keep the lid on things till I get there,

Prentice. I don't want Clarke to foul everything up. The MacCann boy's in a critical condition, you say?'

'They're operating on him tonight. Shall I book our old rooms at the Red Lion, sir?'

'I suppose so. What's the current state of play? Is Eva being charged?'

'Oh, it gets worse, sir. She's saying Cosham's innocent.'

Hayes accepted this with surprising equanimity. After a long pause he merely repeated his instruction to delay Clarke's hand till he got there. The arrival of Mary Ross proved a welcome excuse to evade Hedgecoe's questions and Mo greeted her arrival with muted enthusiasm. 'Just as well you're here, Mary. Inspector Clarke needs a state-ment from you. Sorry we left you in the lurch like that, it was critical to get Eva away and MacCann to hospital immediately.'

'How is he?'

'Not brilliant, but we hope we'll know one way or another by tomorrow.'

'You think he will die?'

Mo shrugged. 'We'll keep our fingers crossed. Was there something, Mary?'

She blurted out her anxieties about the shop and after sympathetic reassurances from Mo, allowed herself to be led to an interview room by Hedgecoe. Just as she reached the door, she turned and scrabbled in her bag. 'Here,' she said, 'I found this on the floor as I was leaving. It's Eva's.'

Mo pocketed the letter and returned to the canteen to pass the time till Hayes rode in like a cavalry charge. She was far from sure how he would take this extraordinary turn of events, confident as he had been to sign off the Brigham case. But now? Two confessions? One attempted suicide? And a knife attack, not to mention one dead horse? She stifled a grin. Hayes hated team games and Clarke would revel in snatching the baton from this know-all of a Met officer.

It proved to be a long night. Eva Brigham insisted on making an official confession as soon as her doctor and the

solicitor hastily pulled in to support her agreed to let her
go ahead. Mo left a sealed message for Hayes with the
sergeant on the desk and, followed by Mary, left at speed.

Mo drove back to Flodde to book their rooms at the Red
Lion and to pick at a late supper while awaiting Hayes'
return. She invited Mary Ross to join her and they were
given a royal welcome by the landlord, whose avid curiosity
had been fed by news about the crazy attack at MacCann's
shop which had already filtered back to the village.

'Mr Wickham's gone, miss,' he said as he laid a table
for them in the snug. 'Took the horses back to Ireland a
week ago. A sad business. Sir William plans to sell up, so
I hear. Can't blame the poor man, can you?'

He chuntered on for several minutes, getting brief replies
from Mo but never a word from the white-faced woman
with her. Mo urged Mary to tuck in. 'You will feel much
better with something inside you. Do you live alone?'

'Since March. I split up with my boyfriend, he got fed
up with my long hours at the shop. Felt neglected.'

'Oh, sorry.'

Mary gave a rueful smile. 'Well, I wasn't too cut up
about it to tell you the truth. He was never going to be the
breadwinner; fancied himself as a rock star and was pissed
out of his mind a lot of the time. You married, Mo?'

'Married to the job, like you.'

The atmosphere lightened as the evening slipped by, and
by the time Mary Ross had sufficiently relaxed to drive
herself home, Mo wondered what was keeping Hayes.

It was after midnight when he finally turned up to join
her in the landlord's back office, where Ted generously set
them up with coffee and yet more sandwiches.

'What gives, Prentice?'

'Nothing new, sir. How did it go with Eva Brigham? Did
you get in on the interview?'

'Bet your boots I did. Luck of the gods you being on the
spot when she went for MacCann. Could turn out to be
murder. Oh, and thanks for that letter. You read it?'

'Mm. Can't say I'm surprised it lit Eva's blue touchpaper.'

'Yeah, a smooth sort of brush-off, all considered.'

'Do you think he guessed about a deal with Cosham?'

He laughed. 'You suppose he worked out that Cosham killed Suzie to give Eva a clean start with her fiancé?'

'Well, MacCann must have realized that Clarke's case against him would never stand up in court. You think there was a conspiracy? He left Suzie knowing Cosham was arriving to kill her?'

Hayes' mouth took a downturn. 'We all got it wrong. Me, you, Clarke and poor bloody MacCann. How's he doing, by the way?'

'Hanging in there. Just. What do you mean, we all got it wrong?'

'Cosham didn't kill anybody.'

Mo slopped her coffee in the saucer, starting up, wide-eyed with excitement.

'I knew it! I meant to tell you, sir. You remember the pathologist said the killer was left-handed? Well, Cosham couldn't have killed Suzie, I saw her sign her statement. It didn't strike me till much later but she's definitely right-handed. Her confession was a fake! And it's just occurred to me, thinking back, seeing Eva strike out at Freddie with the knife. Eva was Suzie's killer, wasn't she?'

Thirty-Six

Hayes pulled out his cigarettes and lit up, his mood inscrutable.

Mo grew impatient. 'Come on, sir, what did she say?'

He drew deeply on the cigarette and exhaled a perfect smoke ring, which hung in the air.

'OK. Here goes. According to Eva, she had just got home from work on the Wednesday night when Zita phoned for her usual chat and dropped the bomb that Denzil, Eva's horse, was being sent back to Ireland. Suzie had confirmed it during a public contretemps with Zita in the post office. Eva hit the roof, causing her mother to wish she had kept her mouth shut until the weekend Eva says, and, frankly, I can feel for poor silly Zita, who must have had previous experience of Eva's volatile temper. Renton is a much more equable sort of guy, from what I've seen of him.'

'Mm. I'd agree with you there, sir. He always struck me as the peacemaker in those awful family rows between Eva and her father.'

'Yeah, well, fired up by fury at Suzie's high-handed decision to send Denzil to the stud farm without so much as mentioning it despite knowing how she loved the beast, Eva flipped. Decided to have it out with Suzie once and for all about the ownership of the horse.'

'But it belonged to Sir William, didn't it?'

'Technically, yes, it did, but Eva guessed Suzie to be the instigator of this plan and I dare say she was right. Suzie was the one who, Sir William knew, had stayed in the marriage – in the beginning anyway – because he could afford to bankroll her stables even if her little pony-club idea went phut.'

'But you can see Eva's point, can't you, sir? She had won prizes with Denzil, having a stepmother push in and take control must have been the killer blow to the armistice the family had agreed prior to her wedding.'

'Well, she explained all that. The interview dragged on, snagged on every damned detail. Clarke has no idea how to stick a suspect to the salient points.'

'I expect he felt Eva would provide a full confession only if he let her have her head.'

'You think so? Rambling on, I'd call it. Anyway, I threw in a spanner every now and then just to keep the ball rolling, and our virago goes on to tell how she caught a late train from London that Wednesday night, bringing her bike along for the extra three miles to the Grange in case the taxi bloke had gone home.'

'She didn't tell Zita she was coming down?'

'No. It was a spur-of-the-moment thing and she biked it to the big house all fired up for a bust-up with Suzie about her horse. It was pouring with rain, just as MacCann said, and as he was pulling away in the MG he caught sight of this woman cycling up the drive in the rain.'

'Not Cosham?'

'Eva.'

'Blimey!'

'Yeah, bad luck all round. Eva sees the MG and realizes that her suspicions about Fred's affair are all too bloody true. Not only was Suzie planning to snatch her horse but had stolen her fiancé, the only man she ever loved.'

'Crikey.'

'Indeed, as you so eloquently phrase it, Prentice. MacCann had just left and when Eva bangs on the door Suzie thinks he's forgotten something I suppose, and comes downstairs shouting, "Just a minute, darling," to let him in. Eva bursts in and, forgetting Denzil, berates Suzie about seducing her man. They argue, the row escalates and stupid Suzie tells Eva to fuck off, turns her back on the girl and makes to go back to bed.'

'Wearing nothing but her gold sandals. Wow. That must have rubbed salt in, knowing Freddie had just left her bed.'

'Too right. Eva grabs the shillelagh from the pot in the hall and chases Suzie upstairs, meaning only, so she says, to make her listen. Fat chance. Suzie trips, loses her shoe, they struggle and Eva loses it totally, her months of frustration and jealousy boiling over in a rain of blows.'

'Suzie was the interloper, of course, sir. She was everything Eva was not: glamorous, sexy, flirty enough to steal the affection of her middle-aged father, wreck the family and, once in control, call all the shots including the disposal of the horses. What did Eva do once she realized the woman was dead?'

'Rushed out of the house and, as Fate would have it, Cosham was passing on *her* bike on the way home after spending an hour at her old home. She grabs Eva, takes a quick dekko at the carnage inside the house, closes the front door and takes Eva back to her cottage to hear the whole story.'

'Eva must have been hysterical.'

'Rigid with shock so she says, allowed Cosham to drag her back to her place, where the two of them collapsed.'

'Eva's clothes must have been horribly bloodstained.'

'Yes, but luckily she'd been wearing her gloves so left no fingerprints. Cosham loved that girl like she was her own, brought her up as a child, could imagine the state Eva must have been in discovering MacCann hot from Suzie's bed like that. Eva said she wanted to call the police, tell them everything, but Cosham had a better plan. She calmed her down, cleaned her up and gave her one of her sister's pills to knock her out for the rest of the night. First thing in the morning she got Eva togged up in her own spare clothes and sent her off to catch the first train back to London and be back at work Thursday morning as usual.'

'Eva fell for this plan? Cosham insisting that now Suzie was out of the picture, Freddie would be back in line and the wedding would go ahead as planned?'

'She convinced the girl that no good would be served by confession, after all there was her poor father to consider, he'd been treated as badly as herself by the wicked stepmother and the family honour was at stake. They both assumed a burglar would be blamed.'

'But MacCann was arrested. How did Eva cope with that?'

'Cosham was the controlling influence throughout, convinced her that he would be released and the wedding need not be cancelled.'

'Cissie Cosham was a cool customer all right. Put Eva back in circulation and kept the truth from the family.'

'The family was Cosham's life. When the plan started to unravel she was prepared to take the blame, serve a life sentence in prison if necessary, just so long as her precious girl got a future.'

'I can't imagine how Eva could let her do that.'

'Eva's an obsessive. First the horse, then MacCann. She flipped when she had to shoot the horse, tried to kill herself and when that failed let Cosham's assurances that MacCann would return to her take hold. He didn't, of course. Freddie MacCann probably guessed the truth and made himself scarce, Suzie's unexpected legacy freeing him from the Brighams for good.'

'And she calmly spelt all this out in the interview room?'

'MacCann's "dear John" letter finally blew it. She really wanted to kill him.'

'What do you think Cissie Cosham will do?'

'It's out of her hands now. Eva's torment wouldn't allow her to carry on with the farce of Cosham's confession after attacking MacCann.'

'But the riding accident was the catalyst.'

'You're right.'

'I bet DI Clarke's over the moon. The press have invaded the town already. It's the sort of crime of passion to go down in the history books.'

Hayes yawned. 'Yeah, well, let's worry about the flak from the media after a night's kip. I've still got to make it good with the Commander that we were never entirely happy with the local police interpretation of the Brigham case. Keep your fingers crossed, Prentice, or we may find ourselves out of a job.'

Thirty-Seven

Three months later Mo returned to give evidence at Eva's trial, a complicated hearing bedevilled with psychiatric reports and intense media interest. After lengthy legal arguments the judge retired to construct his summing-up and advice to the jury.

Mo joined Mary Ross outside and they decided to break through the press cordon and drive to Brighton for supper. Their escape was successfully achieved via Mo's devious back routes and her skilful driving, and they found a small bistro beyond the Lanes which was on the point of opening up for a first sitting. It was called 'The Eyeful', presumably a nod to the Eiffel Tower motif sketched across the window above the cafe curtains.

'Looks quiet,' Mary said with relief, 'and almost empty. I've had enough of telephoto lenses and jostling interviewers, haven't you, Mo?'

'As a police officer I get away with "no comment" but it's been hard for you. Has it affected business?'

They settled at a table set with a gingham cloth and a tiny pot of marguerites. The place was candlelit and already dim, a muted background melody striking a Frenchified ambience.

Mary grinned. 'Actually, the publicity seems to have done me good. Sales are up and not just from people ogling the scene where Eva Brigham all but stabbed her handsome boyfriend to death.' The waiter took their order and they relaxed with a glass of Sauvignon for Mary and a fruit juice for Mo. 'Have you heard anything about Mrs Cosham?'

'Locked up, poor soul, but in an open prison. A short sentence but a criminal record hardly improves one's chances of employment.'

'Will she go back to her sister's place on release?'

'As a matter of fact I heard on the grapevine that Zita Brigham has come up trumps and offered her a home and a job as housekeeper.'

'That's awfully kind. But what about Sir William?' Mo asked.

'Retired. He managed to sell the Grange almost immediately it came on the market but the legal squabble over Suzie's legacy to Freddie is likely to drag on for months. Perhaps Sir William will get back with Zita?'

Mo looked astonished. 'You think so?'

'Well, why not? I expect he's had enough of young brides, and a nice comfortable fall-back with his ex could be very appealing.'

Mo laughed. 'I wouldn't bet on it myself but you may be right, you sentimental thing you. And Renny has stuck by his sister, hasn't he? Never missed a single day in court.'

The waiter served their sole bonne femme and removed the flowers to make space for their side salads and a bottle of sparkling water. They tucked in, the relief of being away from the tense atmosphere of the courtroom sharpening appetites.

'OK, you've managed to keep Freddie's antiques business afloat, Mary, but what's in it for you?'

She raised dark eyes, her mouth twitching with excitement. 'Guess what? Freddie gave me first refusal and I've managed to persuade the bank to back me. I signed the lease last week. The shop's mine!'

Mo crowed with pleasure. 'Oh, Mary, that's terrific! You deserve it, you've got the magic touch. Freddie MacCann was dead lucky having you to keep things running all this time. How's he doing?'

'Really well. Almost fully recovered. He's looking for a place to set up a skiing school in the Alps. And do you know what? Who d'you think's been looking after him since his convalescence?'

'Not Renny Brigham, surely?'

Mary chuckled. 'Nowhere near. It's Tracey. Tracey Wilson.'

'No!'

Mary nodded, her brown curly hair falling about her ears. 'Yes, really. That bloke she was shacked up with—'

'Bill Wickham?'

'Yes, him. Well, he pushed off back to Ireland with the horses and left her flat.'

'Homeless?'

'The staff cottages went with the estate. But Tracey had been visiting Freddie in hospital. He had no one else and the Brighams didn't want to know him, of course, especially since the row over Suzie's will. Little Tracey held his hand and when he moved abroad she went with him.'

'Fell on her feet, then.'

'I think it's a genuine love match. You must have got an inkling of Tracey's good nature during the investigation, didn't you?'

Mo laid down her fork. 'Yes, you're probably right. And when you come to think about it, Tracey's an ideal partner for MacCann. She's practical and a nice kid into the bargain. Not my idea of a typical fortune-hunter at any rate.'

'So?'

'Let's raise a toast to them. Health and happiness to that most unlikely pair, Tracey and Freddie MacCann.'